Clenching his Kalashnikov, the Tamil attacked

He triggered a wild burst, then turned the weapon on himself and chiseled a 7.62 mm hole is his skull.

Now Mack Bolan knew what kind of adversaries he faced. They were so dedicated to whatever cause they served that they would kill themselves rather than risk capture.

The Executioner scouted the immediate area, searching for signs of the fourth gunner. He could see none, but his combat senses warned that he wasn't alone.

The sudden sound of a gunshot made the soldier turn.

A guerrilla lay on the ground, what was left of his face covered by a mask of blood. His limp hands held an AK-47.

A young woman stood over the corpse, holding a .45 Colt Commander in her left hand. She stared at the body, then lifted her head and looked at the big American.

"You missed one, Mr. Belasko," she said calmly.

MACK BOLAN ®

The Executioner

#152 Combat Stretch
#153 Firebase Florida
#154 Night Hit
#155 Hawaiian Heat
#156 Phantom Force
#157 Cayman Strike
#158 Firing Line
#159 Steel and Flame
#160 Storm Warning
#161 Eye of the Storm
#162 Colors of Hell
#163 Warrior's Edge
#164 Death Trail
#165 Fire Sweep
#166 Assassin's Creed
#167 Double Action
#168 Blood Price
#169 White Heat
#170 Baja Blitz
#171 Deadly Force
#172 Fast Strike
#173 Capitol Hit
#174 Battle Plan
#175 Battle Ground
#176 Ransom Run
#177 Evil Code
#178 Black Hand
#179 War Hammer
#180 Force Down
#181 Shifting Target
#182 Lethal Agent
#183 Clean Sweep
#184 Death Warrant
#185 Sudden Fury
#186 Fire Burst
#187 Cleansing Flame

#188 War Paint
#189 Wellfire
#190 Killing Range
#191 Extreme Force
#192 Maximum Impact
#193 Hostile Action
#194 Deadly Contest
#195 Select Fire
#196 Triburst
#197 Armed Force
#198 Shoot Down
#199 Rogue Agent
#200 Crisis Point
#201 Prime Target
#202 Combat Zone
#203 Hard Contact
#204 Rescue Run
#205 Hell Road
#206 Hunting Cry
#207 Freedom Strike
#208 Death Whisper
#209 Asian Crucible
#210 Fire Lash
#211 Steel Claws
#212 Ride the Beast
#213 Blood Harvest
#214 Fission Fury
#215 Fire Hammer
#216 Death Force
#217 Fight or Die
#218 End Game
#219 Terror Intent
#220 Tiger Stalk

DON PENDLETON'S
THE EXECUTIONER®
TIGER STALK

A GOLD EAGLE BOOK FROM
WORLDWIDE.

TORONTO • NEW YORK • LONDON
AMSTERDAM • PARIS • SYDNEY • HAMBURG
STOCKHOLM • ATHENS • TOKYO • MILAN
MADRID • WARSAW • BUDAPEST • AUCKLAND

First edition April 1997
ISBN 0-373-64220-2

Special thanks and acknowledgment to
David North for his contribution to this work.

TIGER STALK

There is no cruder tyranny than that which is perpetuated under the shield of law and in the name of justice.
—Montesquieu (1689-1755)

Those tyrants who hide behind the shield of law are in for a rude awakening when they taste my brand of justice.
—Mack Bolan

THE

MACK BOLAN®

LEGEND

Nothing less than a war could have fashioned the destiny of the man called Mack Bolan. Bolan earned the Executioner title in the jungle hell of Vietnam.

But this soldier also wore another name—Sergeant Mercy. He was so tagged because of the compassion he showed to wounded comrades-in-arms and Vietnamese civilians.

Mack Bolan's second tour of duty ended prematurely when he was given emergency leave to return home and bury his family, victims of the Mob. Then he declared a one-man war against the Mafia.

He confronted the Families head-on from coast to coast, and soon a hope of victory began to appear. But Bolan had broken society's every rule. That same society started gunning for this elusive warrior—to no avail.

So Bolan was offered amnesty to work within the system against terrorism. This time, as an employee of Uncle Sam, Bolan became Colonel John Phoenix. With a command center at Stony Man Farm in Virginia, he and his new allies—Able Team and Phoenix Force—waged relentless war on a new adversary: the KGB.

But when his one true love, April Rose, died at the hands of the Soviet terror machine, Bolan severed all ties with Establishment authority.

Now, after a lengthy lone-wolf struggle and much soul-searching, the Executioner has agreed to enter an "arm's-length" alliance with his government once more, reserving the right to pursue personal missions in his Everlasting War.

1

Mack Bolan looked up at the dark rain clouds that would soon obscure the moon.

He guessed that the humidity was above ninety percent, and even the whistling of the nocturnal birds sounded weak in the moisture-drenched night air.

The big American accepted the discomfort as part of the mission. At least the unceasing rain that was part of the monsoon season hadn't yet arrived. He kept reminding himself that the weather in Sri Lanka was no different than that of most of Southeast Asia.

Night had brought no relief from the humidity. Bolan could feel the one-piece blacksuit he wore clinging to his sweat-soaked body. The black combat cosmetics that covered every inch of his hands and face, right up to the edge of his thick, dark hair, had become runny from the sultry heat.

As a precaution he had stripped off the fatigues he'd worn and stored them in the large canvas carryall he had brought with him. The blacksuit he'd worn under them would make his six-foot-odd frame less visible to any hostiles who might be waiting to attack him.

There was something imposing about the sight of the Executioner in his blacksuit. It was as if he were the agent of death.

For many he had been.

The big American had waited almost an hour for the appearance of the contact who was supposed to meet and drive him to Colombo. He wondered if the woman had been intercepted, and if so, by whom?

The first group that came to mind was the Tamil terrorists who called themselves the Liberation Tigers. Along with the half dozen other dissident ethnic bands who wreaked havoc on the inhabitants, the Tamil terrorists had kept the island nation in a state of war for more than a decade.

Sri Lanka was a country at war with itself, and Bolan knew that no matter who won, everybody lost.

Bolan had come to rescue John Vu. An American of East Indian heritage, skilled at resolving deep-seated issues, he had been accepted as an arbitrator by most parties. But early in the peace process, John Vu had vanished.

The soldier checked his wristwatch. Enough time had passed for any adversaries to search the forest in which he waited and draw him into combat.

Although it appeared that no one had shown up, every nerve in his body set off an alarm that told him he had company. The Executioner couldn't be sure exactly how many, but he was sure they weren't friendlies, and they were waiting for the right moment to attack.

How did they know he was coming and where he would be landing? There was no time to figure that out now. He had to get ready for them.

He checked his artillery: a Beretta 93-R fitted with a sound suppressor sat snugly in a rigid leather shoulder holster; a powerful .44 Magnum Desert Eagle was sheathed in leather at his hip; slung across his right shoulder was a silenced 9 mm Uzi submachine gun; a thin leather sheath strapped to his left forearm had a razor-sharp Applegate-Fairbairn combat knife.

The combat vest he wore contained an ample supply of clips for the Uzi and the pistols. In addition, four M-40 delayed-fuse fragmentation grenades hung from his web belt.

A large canvas carryall at his feet contained more gear, including extra clips for the Uzi, as well as for the Beretta and the Desert Eagle. Additionally, a 5.56 mm M-16 A-2 assault rifle, fitted with an M-203 single-shot grenade launcher, lay beside a small radio transceiver to send messages to the fishing boat waiting in a port in India just across the Palk Strait. An assortment of M-40 and 40 mm fragmentation and incendiary grenades, C-4 plastic explosive, miniaturized detonators, trip triggers and timers, and three compact missile-launching LAW 80s completed the portable armory.

As extensive as his arsenal was, the Executioner had learned from experience that on a mission there was no such thing as being overequipped.

Glancing back at the string of small islets the locals called Adam's Bridge, which connected Sri Lanka and India, he could still see the faint outline of the vessel that had transported him into the area. The captain was a mercenary, asking no questions, but ready to ship cargo, legal or illegal, between India and Sri Lanka. He would be waiting for Bolan's radio signal for a pickup when the mission was completed. That was what he had been paid to do. More cash would change hands when his part was completed.

The only hitch in the escape plan would be the Executioner's death. Then, Bolan knew, it wouldn't matter much where the mercenary sailor waited or fled.

On the crossing from India the crew had studied him carefully, wondering who the big American was, what was in the bag he had brought aboard and why he was sneaking in to Sri Lanka.

The captain, a Tamil from the city of Madras in southeastern India, had tried to engage him in conversation.

"A beautiful country, Sri Lanka. The British called it Ceylon, and while they ruled it, Sri Lanka grew the finest tea in the world." He laughed. "You know the English and their cup of tea. Sri Lanka is the closest thing to paradise on this planet."

Bolan had remained silent. His mind was focused on the mission.

"You probably knew that," the captain continued. "But did you know the Arab traders who landed there called it Serendib, from which the English word *serendipity* comes?"

Bolan had turned to the captain. "Not much serendipity with the Sinhalese and Tamils trying to kill each other."

His blunt comment had ended the captain's attempts at communication.

The Executioner wasn't there to discuss climate or history. He was there to find and rescue a man named John Vu.

The soldier's thoughts were interrupted by the rustling of leaves around him. For a split second he thought it was the evening breeze or a nocturnal animal.

Perhaps it was a roving band of Veddas. There were still pockets of the aboriginal inhabitants of Sri Lanka struggling to survive in isolated corners of the jungle.

Angry with the presence of all invaders and still violent, the Veddas were best left alone.

Tightening his grip on the silenced Uzi SMG in his right hand, the big American scoured the nearby area, searching for signs of life. He spotted two shadows detaching themselves from a shadowy stand of teak trees.

The pair of figures tried to use the jungle brush as a blind while they crouched and worked their way past the banyan tree the soldier was using for cover.

The first of the slender shadows sprinted for the bushes on Bolan's left. The big American could make out the shape of the machete the small man clenched in his hands—and the 7.62 mm AK-47 slung over a shoulder.

Bolan slipped the Applegate-Fairbairn combat knife from its leather sheath, waited patiently until the figure came close, then moved behind a thick stand of foliage. As the attacker moved past him, the soldier clamped a hand over his mouth.

The knife made no sound as it carved a bloody grin across the slender terrorist's throat. Easing the now-still form to the ground, Bolan heard the faintest hint of a noise behind him. Whipping the Beretta from its harness, he spun and loosed a pair of 9 mm rounds that drilled through the second guerrilla's sternum, ruptured one of his lungs and exploded the heart muscle.

Only a short grunt of pain and a small geyser of blood from severed blood vessels announced the end of his life.

The Executioner was in no mood to play cat and mouse with the enemy force hidden in the jungle around him. He didn't know how many there were or where they were hiding.

It was time to flush them.

Moving behind a boulder, Bolan unclipped an M-40 frag grenade from the combat webbing, pulled the pin and lobbed the bomb into the bushes in front of him. Flattening himself against the ground, he could hear the explosion and the shrieks of the dying and wounded as burning shards of metal tore into his hidden assailants.

Tossing a second grenade to his left, Bolan waited for the slivers of burning metal to shred human tissue, then rose and ran twenty yards to his left.

Except for the cries of pain echoing behind him, there was no hint of movement.

The Executioner waited patiently, making sure none of the attackers was watching for him to expose himself. Suddenly the jungle exploded with fury. Automatic weapons opened up from all sides, rounds tearing into the trees and bushes but miraculously missing him.

A slight movement on Bolan's left drew his attention. Two men in fatigues raced into the open space in front of him. He stood and waited for his adversaries to get closer, then hosed the duo with half the rounds in the Uzi's clip. The slugs ripped into the throat of the closer man, nearly severing his head from his body, while the second clutched his midsection, trying to stop his exposed intestines from oozing onto the ground.

As if realizing the effort was futile, the attacker pulled his hands away from his ruptured body and pointed his AK-47 at where Bolan had been standing. In one last, desperate effort, he jammed his finger against the trigger and emptied the clip. The force of the recoil shoved him backward. He fell to the ground and lay there, his blood soaking into the vegetation beneath him.

Battle-wise, the soldier had moved after he had fired his weapon so the slugs from the enemy gunner tore holes into the nearby vegetation.

Bolan wasn't sure who had sent the hit squad, but he knew this wasn't the time to worry about it. Right now he had to find out if there were any of the guerrillas still alive.

He reached into the canvas bag, pulled out a pair of flares, triggered them, then launched them into the air. The area was momentarily bathed with artificial light.

Four shadows ran into the dense underbrush. Weighing his options, the warrior reached into his carryall and dug out a frag grenade. Pulling the pin, Bolan lobbed the bomb into the midst of the four terrorists.

Two terrorists bore the brunt of the shrapnel and crashed to the ground, taken out of play. Cries of agony pierced the quiet night. The Executioner waited until one of his assailants staggered out of the deep brush.

Clenching his Kalashnikov rifle, the Tamil attacker fired wildly, then turned the gun on himself and cored a 7.62 mm hole in his skull.

Now the Executioner knew what kind of adversaries he faced. They weren't good combat soldiers, but were so dedicated to whatever cause they served that they would kill themselves rather than risk capture and its betrayal.

The soldier scouted the foliage surrounding him, searching for any signs of the fourth shadow. He could see none, but some sixth sense warned him he wasn't alone. He moved forward and triggered his Uzi, aiming at the low bush, but there were no cries of pain, no hint of life.

The sudden sound of a gunshot made Bolan turn.

A guerrilla lay on the ground, what was left of his face covered by a mask of blood and torn tissue. His limp hands held an AK-47.

A young woman stood over the corpse, holding a .45 Colt Commander in her left hand. She stared at the body, then lifted her head and looked at the Executioner.

"You missed one, Mr. Belasko," she said calmly.

2

The woman was of Indian descent. Her eyes were classically almond-shaped, but the clothes she wore were modern and utilitarian: jeans and a denim work shirt.

She looked to be in her twenties, though Bolan suspected she was older than that.

The only thing about her he was sure of was that she wasn't an amateur. The way she handled the Colt and her lack of emotion when she looked at the body were telltale characteristics of a professional.

Bolan looked at the gun in the woman's hand. It wasn't aimed at him. He lowered the Uzi gripped in his hand.

"Who are you?"

"Madi Kirbal, a member of the Indian embassy staff in Colombo."

She handed him a small leather folder, containing an ID card with her photo.

Bolan studied it. It was her picture. He knew ID cards could be forged, but a gut feeling told him this one wasn't. She was the contact he was supposed to meet.

Kirbal held out her right hand. Bolan shook it, then got down to business. "I was told my contact was a woman, but that's all."

"I was given your name. Or at least the name you

would be using on this mission, and that's all I was told. Except to give you whatever assistance I could.''

Hal Brognola, Bolan's contact at the Justice Department, had said the woman worked part-time for the American government. The soldier assumed she was getting paid one way or another for meeting him.

Bolan looked at the bodies strewed around the area. ''Tamil Tigers?''

She glanced down at the still-bleeding body on the ground.

''I doubt they were Tigers. If they had been Liberation Tigers, you would not be alive.''

''I thought the Tigers were the main terrorist group.''

''There are other groups, like the Eelam People's Revolutionary Front,'' the woman replied. ''They are Communist led. Of course, they don't go to the bathroom without first checking with their masters in China.''

The conversation was interrupted by a loud whooshing sound. Bolan shoved the woman to the ground and threw himself over her.

''Keep your head down,'' he ordered.

The whining sound traveled past them, and the projectile landed in a grove of banyan trees. The woman started to get up, but Bolan pushed her down again.

''What are you—?''

''Stay down!''

The jungle behind shook with the force of an explosion. Chunks of timber and branches were propelled in every direction by the concussion. Flames began to consume the trees and the brush.

The Executioner watched as the woman got her feet. ''Any injuries?''

Staring in horror at the flaming inferno, the woman replied, "No, I don't think so. How did you know?"

"I've heard the sound before. A fragmentation grenade was launched from a combo launcher-assault rifle."

"So not all of them were dead," Kirbal observed.

"Wait here," Bolan said in a low voice as he hauled the .44 Magnum Desert Eagle from its leather holster. "They soon will be."

"THE GRENADE MUST HAVE killed the American and the woman," the hard-faced guerrilla told his three companions.

"And a lot of the jungle," one of the terrorists commented. "We better tell Colonel Chen that we do not need grenades loaded with so much explosive. The American and the woman could have been killed with a less powerful bomb."

"Perhaps, Kawi. But let us proceed thinking they are still alive," a second fighter suggested.

The third, a young man barely out of his teens, looked puzzled. "What do we do now?"

"Wait."

"For what?"

"Our leader should be here soon. She was delayed in the city of Chilaw for a party meeting."

"Not me," the fourth man said arrogantly. "If they are alive, they are badly injured. We are four. They are only two. I say we finish them off. If need be, I will go by myself."

Reluctantly the other three gave in and gathered their weapons.

"We will search for them in two teams," Kawi said.

The others nodded, then paired up and moved cautiously into the forest.

MACK BOLAN WORKED his way through the jungle, trying to keep the sounds of his movement to a minimum. He placed each foot carefully as he searched for the pocket of adversaries responsible for the attack.

His eyes had become adjusted to the darkness. He could make out and avoid obstacles on the ground. Jungle-warfare experience had sharpened his hearing. Focusing his ears to go beyond the calls of the night birds, the animal coughs and cackling, he listened for sounds of human enemies.

Hushed whispers beyond the stand of teak trees made him stop for a moment. He couldn't make out the words, as his knowledge of the Tamil language was limited. But within minutes he had determined how many guerrillas waited on the other side of the tall hardwood trees. There were two of them, armed, he assumed, with automatic weapons and machetes, if he based the information on the fighters he had already taken out.

Shouldering the M-16 A-2, he eased the Desert Eagle into his right hand. Silence was no longer a consideration. Only death was—his, or the two guerrillas'.

NERVOUSLY THE PAIR of Tamil guerrillas checked carefully behind every tree before moving forward. They had seen the mass slaughter the American invader had wrought on their comrades.

Kawi didn't like not knowing why the American and the woman had to die. Not that he was against killing. He had killed too many to let that bother him.

But he resented that Comrade Diana refused to explain the reason for the ambush.

But he knew better than to argue with the Eurasian woman. He had seen men and women executed for debating party policies.

"It's a matter of loyalty," the British-Sri Lankan woman had snapped when he mentioned his curiosity.

"We will keep our promise to rid Sri Lanka of all capitalists so that the people can run the country. You must keep your commitment to obey orders without question."

The curious Tamil jungle fighter wasn't satisfied with the explanation. But after ten years of guerrilla combat, he wasn't about to try to find a new reason to live.

"Let's follow this trail," Kawi ordered, pointing to a dirt path. "It leads to—"

His words were interrupted by a charging blackclad form.

Before they could shoulder their weapons, Bolan let loose a .44-caliber Magnum round that shattered Kawi's face. Deflected by his jawbone, the lead ricocheted and drove bone splinters into the man's brain.

There was no time for crying out. Death was instantaneous.

The Executioner wasted no time on the new corpse, knowing the man was dead. He made a half turn and fired two rounds into the second guerrilla's heart muscle.

Blood spurted from severed vessels and poured out of the newly created chest cavity.

THE SECOND TEAM of Tamil terrorists heard the explosions and charged toward the sound. The first team had to have found and killed the American.

"It will not hurt our careers if we are there to share in the success," one of the men suggested.

Smiling, the two Tamils gripped their Chinese-made Kalashnikovs and crashed through the bushes.

One of them shouted a question. "Kawi, is the American still alive?"

Mack Bolan was very much alive, and ready for the glory seekers.

The guerrillas stared in horror as they spotted the American. Ramming their AK-47s against their shoulders, they fired wildly, unleashing a torrent of 7.62 mm death.

Bolan had anticipated their movement and darted to the right, the volley of lead shredding branches and leaves, then whining off into the dark.

The soldier turned and faced them. He had to keep one of them alive for questioning.

Two rounds from the Desert Eagle punched into one of the Tamil gunners, driving him backward onto the ground. Verification of death wasn't necessary. Two .44-caliber shots to the head were always fatal.

The big American gestured for the surviving terrorist to drop his weapon. Slowly the guerrilla bent and started to place the carbine on the ground.

Kirbal raised her pistol and fired two rounds in rapid succession. The kill shots drilled into the Tamil's chest and he collapsed to the ground.

"You killed an unarmed man who could have told us who sent him," Bolan growled.

"He would die before he betrayed his cause," she replied coldly, kneeling to remove a chain from around the dead man's neck.

"Thanks to you, he did." Trying to curb his anger, Bolan rammed a full clip into the Desert Eagle.

Kirbal handed him the chain. A cyanide capsule was attached.

"Every Tamil rebel carries one of these around his or her neck. Now you know what we are up against."

3

There was no point arguing with the woman. Bolan wasn't sure why she had shot the fatigue-clad attacker, but perhaps it was to prevent him from telling Bolan what he knew. The one thing he was certain about was that his contact wasn't just trigger-happy.

Either way she was too dangerous to have near him.

"At least there are a dozen Marxists who won't murder any more innocent people," she commented as she led the way along a narrow dirt path.

"They're not the only ones. For every innocent civilian they've killed, I suspect the Tigers have killed fifty," Bolan replied. "And they don't have to get permission from anybody before going out and slaughtering a lot of innocent men, women and children."

"You're oversimplifying a very complex situation," Kirbal protested. "Don't forget that the government has sent out soldiers, the police and their special-task-force butchers to do the same to thousands of innocent Tamils."

Bolan shrugged. He was less interested in domestic politics than in getting his mission accomplished, but he wondered what the Chinese could want in Sri Lanka. The country had no abundance of strategic materials, and the Chinese could buy Sri Lankan tea for a lot less than it had to have cost them to give the guerrilla groups weapons.

He asked the woman to explain it.

"They don't donate their weapons. They sell them. And we know they have agents in Colombo," she countered.

"If you know that, why hasn't the government here found and arrested them?"

"Easier said than done. The Sri Lankan government claims it has its hands full and doesn't have the time to worry about spies. I suspect many government officials get a handsome fee for not seeing what is being smuggled into this country."

"Any likely candidates for top dog?"

"The only prominent Chinese is an importer of Chinese electronic components who has been here for years. Henry Chen. He owns a warehouse on Old Moor Street, near the Pettah bazaar district. But he is a very gentle, cultured man who enjoys such things as classical music and art exhibits."

Bolan studied her. The woman seemed naive about some things, such as how a spy would behave.

Still, she had a strength that impressed him. Madi Kirbal could be a valuable friend or a deadly enemy. He hoped she was the former.

Certainly she was more than just attractive. She was a classic Indian beauty. Her eyelashes were long and silky, her almond-shaped eyes dark and intense. She moved with confidence, like someone who was always in control of the situation and her emotions. Still she seemed passionate about the innocents being destroyed in Sri Lanka. Almost too passionate for someone who wasn't a native.

"You're too good with a weapon to be a simple embassy employee. What are you?"

The woman didn't hesitate. "My full-time post is with Indian Intelligence, the research-and-analysis wing."

The soldier had run into RAW agents in the past. Trained by both the British and Israeli Mossad, the operatives were as resourceful and ruthless as their counterparts in other countries.

"Then why are you here?"

"I was asked by Washington to pick you up and bring you back to Colombo, *and* provide you with whatever information I could."

Bolan waited, but she didn't add anything to the brief explanation.

The young woman had put the .45-caliber handgun she'd carried back into the leather bag that hung from her shoulder. She took out a box of cigarettes and offered one to Bolan. He shook his head, then watched as she put one between her lips and lit it.

"How did you know I was the man you were supposed to meet?"

"You responded to the right name. And, besides, I've been in the field for more than ten years. I've survived by not misjudging my opponents or my allies. I watched you in action before stepping in to help." She paused, then added, "I assume you're CIA."

Bolan didn't correct the Indian Intelligence agent. The truth about his status would only confuse her.

In fact he wasn't officially attached to any government agencies, not even to Stony Man Farm, the antiterrorist organization that Hal Brognola ran. He undertook only those missions in which he believed and where he felt he could make a significant difference.

"From here on out, don't assume anything," Bolan warned. "For instance I could have been someone impersonating Belasko."

"Rebuke acknowledged," the woman allowed. She studied the tall, imposing man who stood before her.

"You remind me of the Vedda, who were here long before the Sinhalese, the Tamils or any of the other ethnic groups. Like you, everything is black and white for them. Reward their friends and destroy their enemies." She paused, then added, "There's one thing more about the Vedda."

"What's that?" Bolan asked.

"Despite a thousand years of invaders trying to wipe them out, the Vedda still survive. Like the aborigines of Australia, they refuse to let civilization erase them or change the way they believe or live. I think you feel the same."

The Executioner was too tired to get into a discussion on the subject. He had been on the move for more than twenty-four hours. What he needed right now was to find his way to the safehouse Brognola had arranged and get a few hours of rest.

"Time to get out of here," he said, looking at the bodies. "Before their friends come looking for them."

"You will like Colombo. It is the most cosmopolitan city in Sri Lanka and one of the most charming cities in the world," Kirbal commented, leading the way to her vehicle.

Bolan had read up on the history of Sri Lanka.

A thousand years of hatred between the Sinhalese and the Tamils simmered, a situation that hadn't been improved by the arrival of the Portuguese, then the Dutch and the British.

The Tigers had begun to emerge in the late fifties when the newly independent nation decided to make Sinhala the official language of Sri Lanka. Discontented Tamils talked about forming their own country, to be called Eelam, so they could follow their Dravidian Hindu teachings.

By 1977 talk had turned to violence, and bands of angry young Tamils began to murder opponents, leaving their brutalized bodies where terrified civilians could view them.

As in Northern Ireland, they claimed religious persecution by the Buddhist majority. A number of hardcore terrorists formed five groups. The most powerful of these was the Liberation Tigers of Tamil Eelam—LTTE, also known as the Tamil Tigers—and the Eelam People's Revolutionary Liberation Front—EPRLF—an extremist Marxist gang.

The government had created a special task force, a group of hardened military fighters to oppose the Tigers and the other rebel groups. The STF answered violence and killings with more violence and even more killings.

Both the government and the Tigers had become more militant in their attitude to each other, and in their actions.

That was the main reason John Vu was asked to get involved.

And, Bolan reminded himself, why he was there. He had to rescue Vu before somebody decided he should die.

If he wasn't dead already.

4

The small, gray-haired man mopped his brow as he paced the confined sandstone room. He checked for ways to leave but could find none. There were bars on the windows, and the door was bolted from the outside. Even the morning sun had a hard time reaching into the prison cell.

The furnishings were sparse: a toilet and sink, a narrow bed and a table with four chairs.

There was no telephone, no television, no radio.

Several pamphlets sat on the table. Most were in Tamil, but one was in English. It was an explanation why the Tigers had to resort to violence to save their people.

John Vu had read the pamphlet a dozen times. If his captors thought it would brainwash him, they were wrong. He had been confronted by more persuasive politicians and lobbyists when he was undersecretary of state, and none of them could get him to change his mind once he made a decision.

The basic necessities had been provided in the past several days, food, bottled water and a small quantity of tobacco for his worn pipe.

If the Tigers were trying to get him to convince the Sri Lankan government to turn the Jaffna peninsula into a Tamil-controlled, independent country, they were wasting their time.

The negotiator operated on common sense. The Tigers wouldn't be satisfied with the peninsula. Soon they would demand more land, then more, until they were strong enough to demand control of the entire country.

The door opened. A guard pointed a Russian-made PSM autoloader at him.

In broken English he ordered Vu to go with him.

"The commander wishes to talk to you."

He was pleased. The sooner the two of them could come to an understanding, the sooner he could get back to the negotiating table.

KIRBAL LED THE WAY through the brush to where she had parked her vehicle. Bolan followed close behind, hauling the heavy carryall. The Desert Eagle was back in its holster, fitted with a fresh magazine. The silenced Uzi SMG was slung over a shoulder.

Pausing to listen for sounds that might indicate the presence of a still-living assailant, the soldier heard nothing but the whistling of night birds.

Fifty yards ahead of them was a British Land Rover.

Bolan kept looking around for signs of life.

Kirbal turned and stared at him. "Is something wrong?"

"Yeah. I understand this forest preserve is supposed to be patrolled by armed rangers. Where were they when we were fighting the guerrillas?"

"When you are in a war zone, all you can hope to do is stay alive. The rangers almost never go out at night. Even in daytime they travel only in large, heavily armed groups."

The Executioner threw his canvas bag into the rear of the vehicle, then slid into the passenger seat.

"Looks like my mission has been compromised. No one but you was supposed to know I'm here," Bolan commented. "Apparently a lot of people know."

"It seems so," the woman agreed. "Would you like me to arrange transportation for you to leave Sri Lanka?"

"Not until John Vu is safely home. I'm guessing that the Tigers are holding him captive."

"They don't usually resort to kidnapping foreign diplomats," Kirbal commented.

"There's a first time for everything."

A noise from behind some bushes grabbed the soldier's attention. He unslung the Uzi then, signaling for Kirbal to wait in the car, silently worked his way around the far end of the thick vegetation.

THE TAMIL LEADER was waiting in a small office. When Vu entered and extended his hand, the gray-haired man in fatigues ignored it.

"Sit here, Mr. Vu," he said coldly, pointing to a small wooden chair in front of his metal desk.

Vu noted the large map of the island nation mounted on the wall behind the desk. The northern portion had been highlighted by a different color than the rest of the country.

"At least you know my name," he commented, forcing a smile on his face. "I don't know yours."

"Not that it matters, but they call me Thamby. It means 'little brother' in Tamil."

The man behind the desk wore a holstered Hungarian copy of the 9 mm Browning Hi-Power M-1953 GP, which he kept fingering.

"We know a great deal about you, Mr. Vu," said Rajiv Thamby, one of the three Tamils who made up the high command of the Tigers. "We know about your former government position, your personal life and your military history."

"Well," Vu said, trying to sound casual, "I guess you went to a lot of trouble finding out about me."

"No, we have friends in many places. What we don't know is who you really represent."

"That's simple. The President of the United States asked me to talk to all sides in this dispute and see if I could find some basis on which peace could be achieved."

"Are you CIA, Mr. Vu?"

The elderly man laughed. "Do I look like a spy?"

"Spies come in all sizes and colors. And," Thamby added, "all ages."

"No," Vu assured him, "I'm not CIA. Technically I'm nothing but an ordinary citizen who has come to see how he can get you all to stop killing one another. Just tell me what it is you want. That would be a start."

The gray-haired Tiger leader got up from his chair and walked to the map behind him. "What we want is simple." He ran his index finger around the perimeter of the highlighted area on the map. "We want all of this for our own country. We will call it Eelam."

"Okay. That's what you want. What will you settle for?"

"The same thing. If we are offered anything less, we will continue to protect our rights as Tamils no matter how many have to die."

Vu got up from his chair.

"I guess that's what I'll have to tell the Sri Lankan government."

He started to walk toward the door.

"You will tell them nothing," the Tamil said.

Vu stopped and turned to look at Thamby.

"You may make a tape with our offer, but you will stay here until we have gotten a reply to our demands."

THE FATIGUE-CLAD WOMAN had watched the slaughter silently, only her dark eyes revealing the fury she felt at the incompetence of her men.

"Let's take the American alive. We can turn him over to the colonel for questioning, Comrade Yasmine," the guerrilla at her side said, showing her the AK-47 he was holding. "This should convince him."

Checking the clip of the Czech-made Skorpion SMG she had been given as a reward for her many successful attacks on the enemies of the people, she nodded her approval of the attack and started to ease her way through the bush. There was a rustle behind her, then came the order.

"Drop the gun!"

It was the American, gripping the stubby SMG in his right hand.

The small man in fatigues at her side reacted to the command with an ill-aimed burst of rounds. None hit the Executioner.

Bolan cut down the terrorist with a short burst from the Uzi, then focused his attention on the woman.

"Drop the gun," he repeated.

As he waited for her to comply, she offered a cold smile of hate and tightened her finger on the trigger.

The negotiations were over.

He fired a trio of rounds. Two of them tore into her side before she could fire back. The third destroyed her left kneecap.

Blood colored her camouflage uniform. Despite being in obvious pain, she tried to shoot back.

"Don't," Bolan warned.

Stubbornly she kept trying.

There wasn't time for pity. As the terrorist leveled her weapon, Bolan let loose another short burst that punched her to the ground.

He turned to head out, but some instinct made him whirl. Another terrorist stood behind him, another woman, younger than the first but just as deadly.

Her eyes were filled with hate. "You are prisoner," she spit in fractured English. "Drop weapon."

Bolan lowered the Uzi, trying to figure how to stay alive.

Shots rang out from behind the female guerrilla. She fell forward, dead, the rounds from her assault rifle tearing into the ground. Madi Kirbal lowered her weapon and walked forward to join Bolan. Neither said a word as they walked out of the jungle and got into her vehicle.

The woman reached under her seat and took out an envelope. "I was asked to prepare a situation report for you. The names of some of the major players, and their involvement in the current crisis, are included."

"Later. First we have to get out of here in one piece."

Kirbal saw the grim determination in the soldier's face and slid behind the wheel.

"Agreed," she replied as she started the engine and shifted gears.

He looked down at her lap, which held her .45-caliber Colt Commander.

"Do you always drive with a loaded weapon in your lap?"

"Only when I'm in a war zone," the woman replied bluntly.

The Executioner knew she was right. This was a war zone, and he had invited himself to join in the battle.

5

The weathered sign on the front door of the compact one-story warehouse on Old Moor Street read Shanghai Trading Company. Inside, cartons of merchandise were stacked high in the storage area.

A sliding wall divided the area into two. The other half was only half-filled with wooden crates marked Electronic Components. Inside the boxes were thousands of rounds of ammunition for the Chinese-made AK-47s, as well as cases of grenades and rockets.

A glass-paneled door stood at the far end of the stone-and-metal building.

Inside the office, a clean-shaved Oriental in his early fifties sat behind the plain wooden desk, his fingers locked together. The soft, neatly ironed cotton shirt and linen pants he wore couldn't mask his military posture.

As if he were viewing some distant object, Colonel Chen kept staring at the simple painting on the far wall. He had much to consider.

He had already known about the negotiator who had arrived from America, but the man had vanished before he could have him assassinated.

And a fishing-boat captain had notified him that he had been hired to smuggle an American into the country. Obviously the U.S. was meddling again, sending a CIA agent to hunt for the diplomat.

He suspected that the efforts of the negotiator could be successful. Both the Sri Lankan government and the Tamil Tigers had become weary of the mass killings.

Even his own Communist-led EPRLF guerrillas had started defecting and returning to their villages in the north of the country.

He had to find a way to stop any truce from becoming a reality. Those were his instructions from the Ministry of State Security in Beijing. Peace would end the efforts to turn Sri Lanka into an ideal Communist country, and, more immediate, would hurt the sale of Chinese-made arms to the various antigovernment groups.

A practical man, Colonel Chen had spent the past fifteen years maintaining relations with all of the terrorist groups. Over the years many of their leaders were smuggled out of the country and into China to undergo military training. The only commitment they'd had to make was to purchase their weapons from his country.

A ship filled with weapons for the rebels was waiting to be unloaded at a small dock north of Colombo. The cargo was consigned to the Tigers. Even if they weren't Communists, Chen was pleased to sell them arms.

Anything to keep the Sri Lankan government in turmoil.

He would let nothing interfere with that goal, which was why he'd had Major Sung send a force of revolutionaries north to meet the American agent sent to find the missing diplomat. Fortunately the fishing-boat captain had told him where and when he would land.

What was the name of the agent? Colonel Chen searched through a small stack of papers for his notes and found it: Michael Belasko.

The Chinese Intelligence official smiled, certain that the name was created for the mission. Most likely the man was with the CIA.

His personal terrorist squad, the Eelam People's Revolutionary Liberation Front, was at this moment waiting in ambush to kill this Belasko.

The next step was to find the diplomat who had come to Sri Lanka as a mediator and send him to join his ancestors.

Chen began to scribble a list of names on a pad. It would take the efforts of all the forces he had in Sri Lanka to locate the negotiator and the Tigers entertaining him. He would have Major Sung make the contacts as soon as he returned.

There was a soft knock on the door. It was late. The warehouse workers had all left, as had his secretary, May Ling, an attractive young woman who even now was waiting for him at his house outside of the city.

Unless he was mistaken, the knock belonged to Major Sung, the new aide Beijing had sent to assist him. Probably the man had returned to gloat about his first major victory in Sri Lanka.

But, he reminded himself, a careful man never took unnecessary risks. Chen opened his desk drawer and eased out a pistol, placing it on his lap.

"Enter, please," he called, then pretended to scan some documents.

Sung entered, his eyes filled with fear.

"I bring sad news, Colonel."

Sighing, the gray-haired man set down his notes and looked up. "What great tragedy has occurred that couldn't wait until morning?"

"The forces we sent are dead. When I got no radio message, I contacted one of our people who works in the Whelped National Park. He drove to where the American was supposed to land, but all he found were the bodies of the men who were supposed to stop the mercenary."

"The American?"

"I presume he is alive. So is the woman."

"So *your* men failed."

Sung knew better than to argue. Colonel Chen was both ambitious and vindictive.

"I hang my head in shame at their inadequacy," the younger man said, feigning a humble tone.

Chen stared icily at his subordinate. "So all we know is that he had come to Sri Lanka on some secret mission."

"We assume that is why he is here, Colonel," Sung replied defensively.

"When a man sneaks into a country without going through normal channels, you can do more than assume he is not here for a vacation," Chen replied sarcastically.

"But is he here because the American negotiator has vanished?"

"I will ask him when you capture him and bring him to me." He sighed. "This is indeed sad news, Major Sung." He paused. "For all you know, he has found the missing negotiator and is getting ready to take him out of the country." The words came as a thinly veiled accusation.

The young major started to perspire. "We will pick up the search again in the morning."

"Meantime many of our Marxist brothers have been murdered by this capitalist American."

Sung cringed. Colonel Chen was the local intelligence chief for the Ministry of State Security. The MSS was responsible for espionage. This was Sung's first mission out of China, and he had already failed miserably.

Chen hammered another question at the younger man. "Do we at least know where he was going?"

Sung's voice cracked as he replied. "We...I think his destination was Colombo. At least that's where the Americans have their embassy."

"How would he get here?"

"Our man found tire tracks that led to the main road."

"So you assume this American is heading for the American Embassy here. And he is alone."

"I...think so."

"And there is one major highway that connects Whelped National Park and this city?"

"Yes. Highway 3."

"Then it doesn't really matter why he is here. Gather some men and stop him before he arrives."

The young man turned to leave, then stopped. "How many men?"

The senior intelligence officer let his exasperation show.

"How many will it take to stop him?"

"I don't know. Two or three?"

"He killed more than a dozen men tonight. I suggest you take at least that many. Perhaps more."

"Yes, sir."

"And arm them properly this time," the colonel snarled.

THE SHORT, HEAVYSET MAN reached across his large desk and pushed the intercom.

"Get me Colonel Pratap," he ordered brusquely.

As he waited for his secretary to complete the call, Allan Bandaran drummed his fingers on his desk. Despite the special dehumidifier he'd installed, he could feel perspiration soaking the armpits of his carefully ironed white shirt. The moisture had begun to soak into his impeccably tailored suit.

He could hardly contain his rage. How dare the Americans send one of their diplomats to his country to talk to the Tamils? This was purely an internal matter. And he, as minister of internal security, was solely responsible for maintaining the peace—even if it meant killing a lot of the Tamil trash to achieve it.

It had been a difficult morning since that first call from Simon Alphamundai.

"Allan, this diplomat the Americans sent several days ago has vanished," the cold, formal voice had reported.

"What diplomat, Mr. President?"

"John Vu. He came here to see how he could help us establish better relations with the Tamil revolutionaries."

Bandaran was stunned. "You knew this and didn't tell me? I thought he was just on a goodwill tour."

"His government asked that his presence as anything but a tourist be kept quiet. We depend on the United States for both assistance and trade. I saw no need to violate their confidence."

"And now we have a kidnapping on our hands.

Probably done by those damned Tigers," Bandaran growled.

"I am ordering you to send out every man you can spare and find him. Alive. If he is killed, the entire country will be shamed in the eyes of the world. Not just the Tamil rebels."

"What happens if we find him alive?"

"Then perhaps we can finally achieve peace," the Sri Lankan president said, and hung up.

The rest of the day had passed no better. Bandaran was too preoccupied to care. He could see his sizable side income shrinking to almost nothing if the American diplomat was able to achieve his true purpose for coming to Sri Lanka.

Just as he slammed his fist on the desk in rage, the phone rang. Bandaran snatched it from the cradle and growled into the speaker.

"Pratap?"

"Yes, Minister."

"We have a problem. A serious one. Free up your schedule. I'm driving to your camp for an in-person conference."

He slammed down the phone and forced his paunchy body from the leather chair. Suddenly he felt older than his fifty-seven years. If things continued to go so badly, he might have to resign and live off the money he had carefully set aside in Zurich.

BOLAN AND KIRBAL had been driving for two hours. The highway to Colombo was poorly lit. Long stretches of forest lined Highway 3, interspersed with the outskirts of small cities, an occasional village and countless Buddhist shrines.

As they drove, Madi Kirbal wondered how the Chinese "importer" would react when he heard that more than a dozen of his private army troops had been killed in battles with Belasko.

She had called Thamby to tell him about being ordered to assist the American.

Not only was Rajiv Thamby one of the triumvirate that ruled the Liberation Tigers, but he was also her lover. Her obsession for him had turned her into someone she never imagined she'd become.

Because of him and her loyalty to her mother's Sri Lankan family, she had violated her oath of allegiance to the Indian government and become an informer for the rebel cause.

That she was also betraying the Americans didn't bother Kirbal. Blood and love were thicker than water, even if American blood would flow before this episode was finished.

Thamby had agreed that she should assist the American until he was done talking to the diplomat.

The Tamil commander had added one more order. "My sister, Sirimavo, was kidnapped by the special task force when they raided her village. She is one of the thousands living in squalor at the Boosa Camp. Suggest to the American that if he rescues her, she might be willing to tell him where to find me—and the diplomat he seeks."

She was skeptical. "Isn't that dangerous?"

"Except for a few trusted friends, nobody knows Sirimavo is my sister, and she would rather die than betray the cause."

"What if she does tell him, or your talks with the negotiator fail?"

"Then I will kill the diplomat and I will expect you to do the same with the American Intelligence agent."

The thought of killing the man sitting next to her bothered Kirbal. Not that she had a rational explanation for how she felt.

He was different from most other men. As cold and precise as he appeared, there was a compassion for people inside he couldn't hide. She felt sadness knowing that he would have to be killed, probably by her.

Bolan's voice brought her back to the present. "Something bothering you?"

"No, not at all. I was thinking about the innocent people who have died because of the war between the rebel liberationists and the government."

Kirbal tried to pass on some of the background to the Sri Lankan conflict to the American sitting next to her.

"You will hear that the war between the Tamils and the Sinhalese is based on different religious beliefs. To some degree that is true. For the most part the Sinhalese are devout Buddhists. Legend has it that a branch of the bo tree under which Buddha sat to gain enlightenment was brought to this country and planted in the north. Who really knows?

"The Tamils, on the other hand, are of the Dravidian Hindu faith." She smiled cynically. "Ironically both the Tamils and the Sinhalese originally migrated to Sri Lanka from India."

The soldier only half listened. He was busy keeping a wary eye out for possible ambushes. Lonely stretches of highway were likely places for attacks by some hidden enemy. But he had heard enough of the RAW agent's comments to ask, "If not religion, why the hatred and violence?"

"As in every other country in the world, it's a matter of political power and money. The Sinhalese control the government and will not share their power or wealth. Most Tamils work on tea plantations or in factories. Some run small shops. But there are no rich Tamils.''

"Then who pays for the Tigers' weapons?''

Kirbal shook her head. "No one really knows. Some say the funds come from Tamils who live in India, just across Adam's Bridge. Others claim the backing must come from foreign governments who think they can control the fate of Sri Lanka by helping to arm the Tigers.''

The Executioner made a face and asked a pointed question. "Like the Indian government?''

"We tried that a number of years ago. We sent in a peacekeeping force, but maintaining even a semblance of peace almost bankrupted the government. The other foreign powers will learn that no one controls the fate of this country except those who live here,'' the Indian woman replied, then leaned forward and focused her attention on the empty road.

"What about the special task force?''

Kirbal shook her head. "They are the power that keeps the government in office. They run their own troops, maintain their own armories, train their own soldiers, run their own prison camps and execute anybody they think is against them.

"The government formed the STF to fight the terrorists. They took their best soldiers and sent them abroad to learn from experts how to kill those who disagreed with them. Then they hired mercenaries to help the STF slaughter innocent men, women and even children.''

"Who runs the STF?''

"The actual operations are run by a general staff in

Colombo, headed by a team of officers. The most vicious is a Colonel Pratap, who runs their largest prison camp, just south of Colombo. The Boosa Camp is the worst in all of Sri Lanka. Pratap has thousands of Tamil prisoners, none of whom has ever had a trial. His men are free to abuse the prisoners—especially the women—without threat of punishment. His personal taste, I am told, runs to young boys.

"But the real power is the minister of internal security, Allan Bandaran, who's half British, half Sinhalese. He is an Oxford-educated politician who has his finger in every illegal business in the country. Eliminate people like Bandaran and Pratap—and the religious fanatics who back them—and you've gotten rid of much of what is wrong with this country."

"So a lot of innocent people are killed, just because they're the wrong faith, ethnic type or in the wrong location," Bolan replied. "Hitler, Saddam Hussein, the Ayatollah and a lot of men like them used to hire people who enjoyed seeing decent people suffer."

Bolan studied various structures as they drove past them. Several villas surrounded by high stone walls appeared, but for the most part the houses were huts held together with little more than prayer.

Something made his skin tingle, a sense of danger ahead. He had survived too long to ignore the warning signals.

"Pull to the side of the road," he ordered.

The RAW agent misunderstood the reason for his command. "If you can wait a half hour, there is a small restaurant with rest-room facilities."

"Now!"

Surprised at the harshness in his voice, Kirbal pulled

off the road, stopped the Land Rover, and turned to him.

"Is something wrong?"

The soldier tried to listen past the usual night sounds. Nothing.

Reaching for the canvas bag, he took out the M-16 A-2 and several clips, which he shoved into the pockets of the combat vest. Checking the clip of the carbine, he snapped in a fresh magazine and jacked the first round into the chamber. Then he loaded an incendiary grenade into the M-203 launcher mounted beneath the powerful assault rifle. Not only was the M-16 A-2 capable of pouring 800 rounds of high-velocity 5.56 mm ammo per minute at a muzzle velocity of 1000 feet per second, but the launcher made it possible to hurtle a 40 mm grenade accurately as far as 400 yards.

Seemingly satisfied, Bolan started to rise, then changed his mind and reached into the bag again. As he brought out a long tube, the woman, who'd been watching him, recognized the weapon.

"Why on earth would you need a LAW right now?"

"I might not," Bolan replied, slinging the antitank rocket over a shoulder, "but I always like to be prepared for anything." He nodded to the woman. "Let's get going."

As the woman resumed driving, Bolan could feel the heat of tension radiating from her.

"It may be nothing," he said, trying to reassure her, "but if there is an attack, follow my orders immediately. Every second you delay may cost us our—"

The rest of his sentence was punctuated by automatic gunfire coming from both sides of the road.

"Get this car into the woods," he shouted, hefting the M-16.

6

Without hesitation Kirbal spun the steering wheel hard and plunged into an open space in the bushes. The Land Rover bucked as it bounced on the uneven forest ground, but she managed to hold on to the steering wheel.

"Stop," Bolan shouted.

Stepping hard on the brake, she managed to stop the vehicle, causing it to stall.

"Get out and find cover," Bolan told her.

Gripping the Colt in her right hand, Kirbal threw herself behind a wide banyan tree. Glancing at where she had taken refuge, the soldier decided she was safe for the moment.

With determination he pushed his way into the thick vegetation and moved toward the source of the gunfire. Two fatigue-clad assailants had their backs turned to him.

The sound of a small branch breaking made them spin. Each man had a firm grip on a Chinese-made 7.62 mm Type 85 light submachine gun. At the sight of the big American, the hardmen squeezed the triggers.

Bolan had anticipated their actions. Dodging to the left like a fullback avoiding a tackler, he fired a burst of 5.56 mm bullets at the closer of his adversaries.

The rounds carved a path through the terrorist's neck and up into his brain, killing him instantly.

The second terrorist recovered quickly from the shock of seeing his comrade torn apart, and quickly emptied the magazine of his weapon at Bolan. But the Executioner had twisted out of the line of fire and heard the rounds smack into the trunk of a tree behind him.

While the Tamil tried to force a fresh magazine into his weapon, Bolan turned his M-16 on the man and swept his carbine in a deadly figure eight.

Looking down at the cavity where his stomach and digestive organs had been minutes earlier, the dying fighter saw the blood from his body wash over his hands, then sat down abruptly and waited for death to claim him.

Scanning the nearby woods for hidden enemies, Bolan sensed the presence of a large force on both sides of the highway. He knew he could stand and fight, but he had a more important task ahead of him.

It was time to retreat.

Kirbal emerged from behind the tree and ran to him. "Are they all dead?"

"No, but it's time we got out of here."

As they approached the Land Rover, Bolan stopped. "Get the car started. I'll be there in a minute."

Kirbal started to argue with him, then changed her mind. She had known him only a few hours, but already she trusted his combat judgment.

The soldier listened for a moment, then, focusing carefully through the sight mounted on the left, adjusted the setting. Squeezing the trigger on the M-203 grenade launcher, he watched as the metal missile traveled above the treetops, then turned and ran for the vehicle as the grenade exploded.

The woman started to get out to let him take over the wheel.

"You drive," Bolan directed. "I might be busy keeping us alive."

Getting behind the wheel of the vehicle, the woman waited until Bolan got in, then started the engine and floored the gas pedal.

As the Land Rover began to race in the direction of Colombo, a hail of autofire chased them down the highway. But disoriented by the grenade, the ambushers were too late, and their fire was high and wide.

"That takes care of that group," Kirbal commented in a calmer voice.

"We're not there yet," Bolan warned.

As if his words had been a prophecy, an armored personnel carrier lumbered out of the woods in front of them.

Bolan recognized it as a Chinese copy of the Soviet BTR-40. Sitting above the driver in a small swivel seat, a fatigue-clad guerrilla squinted carefully through the sight of the 7.62 mm RP-46 machine gun.

"Weave!" Bolan shouted.

Responding instantly, the woman swerved the Land Rover so their path was erratic.

A steady stream of lead pumped from the mounted machine gun, missing the Land Rover and its occupants by scant inches.

"The gunner's getting too accurate. Into the woods!"

"Can't we outrun him?"

"Not with the range of that machine gun. And we

don't know what other kinds of weapons they're carrying.''

Kirbal drove the vehicle off the road and headed for a clearing in the underbrush.

Bolan jumped from the truck before she stopped it.

"I'll be back," he promised.

MAJOR SUNG OPENED the armored door to the roof of the APC and stared up at the gunner.

"Why did you stop firing?"

"They ran into the forest, Comrade Sung," the gunner explained.

"We will follow them."

As the driver spun the wheel of the armored vehicle, Sung reached down and picked up a flamethrower.

"We'll burn them out, or they can stay hidden and roast to death," he commented as he hefted the bulky weapon.

Twenty yards ahead of him he could see the faint outline of the British-made vehicle hiding behind some banyan trees.

"Stop here," he ordered, and got out when the carrier came to a halt.

"Maintain a stream of fire on the Land Rover," Sung ordered.

The weight of the bulky flamethrower made the major stoop slightly. He opened the valves and ignited the narrow tips, adjusting the flame until it sprayed a long stream of fire in front of him.

Then he walked slowly toward the Land Rover behind a steady spray of fiery destruction. Trees and bushes ignited, sending clouds of smoke skyward. The frightened sounds of birds fleeing the area echoed in the sky.

"Colonel Chen will be pleased with our success," he proclaimed proudly.

BOLAN HAD SLIPPED behind the trees until he had a clear view of the BTR-40. Slipping the LAW from his shoulder, he pulled the safety pin. The end caps fell away, and the weapon telescoped another six inches while it armed itself. The missile launcher carried a 66 mm round with a hollowpoint nose, shaped like a small teacup. The whole unit weighed about five pounds.

Sighting through the eyepiece that moved into position on top of the launcher, Bolan saw the flames spitting from the shoulder-mounted thrower. Momentarily surprised that the guerrilla seemed to be Chinese, the soldier knew he had to move fast and accurately or he and his companion would be charred memories.

Focusing on the APC, he pulled the trigger and mentally crossed his fingers. The missile raced out of the tube at a speed of almost 500 feet per second and cut a hole through the BTR-40 as if it were made of paper.

He could hear the missile exploding with the deafening sound of thunder, tearing the armored vehicle in two. Molten bits of metal from the warhead and flames shot back at him, scorching trees in their path.

Over the exploding ammo, Bolan could hear muffled screams as superheated chunks of metal and flame consumed the men in and around the APC. The smell of burning flesh fouled the air, making him feel nauseous.

He waited for the intense heat to dissipate, then worked his way back to the Land Rover. He hoped Kirbal had not been injured in the swift battle.

She was waiting for him, crouching on the floor of the vehicle. She started to raise the Colt Commander, then lowered it when she realized it was Bolan.

"Next time I will go with you," she snapped. "I felt like a helpless bystander watching a war being fought."

Getting into the vehicle, Bolan pointed to the wheel. "Drive. It's been a very long thirty-six hours."

The Executioner had arrived, and the terrorists had been taught a lesson about killing.

7

Denzil Pratap sat in the custom-built leather chair behind his desk and listened as the minister of internal security described his problem. The man stared down at Allan Bandaran. He'd had the furniture maker add four inches of height to his seat so he appeared taller to those who stood or sat in front of his desk.

"We need to find out where the Tamils are holding the negotiator," Bandaran insisted.

"How can I be of assistance?"

"You must have someone among the thousands of Tamils who would have an idea where the Tigers would take such a man."

Without a word the camp chief lifted the phone and summoned the person on the other end to come to his office.

A tall, wide man in a STF uniform entered the office. His mouth was twisted into a permanent smile, the result of battle wounds that had paralyzed his facial muscles.

"Sergeant Dharvin Raja is in charge of interrogation," Pratap told his visitor.

Briefly the colonel outlined the problem.

"We have questioned almost a hundred of them," the bull-like noncom commented. "All of them died before we could find the right kind of questioning to get them to talk.''

"There is a young Tamil woman we are holding here,'' Pratap said. "Her name is Sirimavo. She is the youngest sister of one of the three leaders of the Tamil terrorists, the man who calls himself Thamby.''

Raja looked surprised. "I did not know, Colonel. None of the men or women I questioned said anything about her.''

Bandaran exploded. "Why wasn't I notified about her?''

"I only just found out, Minister,'' Pratap replied calmly. "A call came from a Tiger informant who is willing to trade information to ensure his mother is treated well in the camp.''

"Have you questioned her about where her brother is hiding?''

"I talked to her,'' Pratap admitted. "She even refused to acknowledge that she is the Tiger terrorist's sister.''

"It is essential to get her to tell us where to find Thamby.''

"Do I have your permission to use any means to get the information?''

"Just remember that we are not animals like the Tigers.''

The camp commander looked at the sergeant and nodded his unspoken approval to use any means to get the woman to talk.

IT WAS ALMOST MIDNIGHT before they reached the city. As they drove through the brightly lit downtown section of Colombo, dodging cars, buses, trucks and pedicabs, Bolan studied the pedestrians. The streets were filled with them: tourists, the wealthy, police and army patrols and prostitutes.

There wasn't a corner devoid of young women selling their bodies.

Poverty bred prostitution, and Sri Lanka had become a poor country since the conflict between the Sinhalese and the Tamils had started.

"What do you know about contraband arms being smuggled into the country tomorrow night?" Bolan asked. "Do you know who deals in contraband?"

"It could be one of a dozen men. The minister of internal security, Mr. Allan Bandaran, for one," Kirbal answered.

Bolan didn't look surprised. He had encountered politicians who used their positions to accumulate wealth, and had confronted many of them.

"Mr. Bandaran likes the things money can buy. And he gets a commission for every shipment of illegal arms brought into Sri Lanka, with little exception. But I'm certain that your information about tomorrow night is incorrect. I would have heard."

The Indian agent dug out a formal-looking business card from her purse and wrote a telephone number on it.

"Call me when you're free," she suggested.

As they stopped for a red light, she looked at the soldier and asked, "Where can I drop you?"

Bolan looked out of the rear window. They weren't being followed. "At the nearest cabstand."

"There are barricades all over the city. I can take you part of the way. You'll have to walk the rest. Or if you drop me at my home, you can borrow my vehicle," she offered.

"What if you need your car before I can return it?"

"There is another one I can use. A government vehicle. I have to return it to our embassy car pool anyway."

As she directed him to her apartment complex, she fed him the information Thamby had given her.

"There is one thing more I heard. Thamby has a sister named Sirimavo. She is being held by the STF at its prison camp south of Colombo."

"I'm surprised they haven't tortured her to find out where Thamby is hiding," Bolan commented.

"They don't know she is his sister." She studied the soldier for a long time. "I don't think they will find it out from you. Not even if it meant your life."

The Executioner nodded. He'd acquired the nickname Sergeant Mercy many years earlier because, while he killed those who were his enemies, he went out of his way to help the innocent and lead them to safety.

"If I can, I'll make sure she is returned to her family," he promised.

THE NEXT MORNING Kirbal made sure she wasn't being followed, then got out of the small Volkswagen cab she had called. She walked around to the rear of a sandstone building on Chatham Street, checked the contents of her large handbag, then entered a door.

Inside was a small commercial bank, the Colombo branch of the National Industrial Bank of India.

Without stopping, she walked unnoticed down a narrow corridor to a carved wooden door, fitted with a glass panel, and opened it.

The man behind the desk was in his early sixties. A tall, stately-looking man with a shock of pure white hair, Ravindra Lal looked and sounded more like a member of the Indian diplomatic corps than an Indian intelligence officer.

He glanced up and nodded his acknowledgment of her presence, then went back to studying a single sheet of paper covered with typewritten words.

To the business community of Colombo, Lal was a banker. The title on the closed wooden door proclaimed that he was the manager of the branch.

For more than twenty years, Lal had handled the financial needs of Indian clients doing business in Sri Lanka. To the attractive young woman who had taken the liberty of pulling a leather chair closer to his desk and sitting in it, he was much more than that. He was her superior, the head of the research-and-analysis wing of Indian Intelligence in Sri Lanka.

"We can talk frankly and without interruption?"

Kirbal looked over her shoulder to make sure no one was peering in through the glass panel in the wooden door.

"As you may remember from your last visit, no one will disturb us as long as my door is closed," he reminded her.

He smiled and pointed to a couch. "Wouldn't you be more comfortable there?"

She glanced around the room. It was furnished with English period pieces: a Hepplewhite cabinet, Queen Anne chairs and tables, a large display case crowded with antique porcelain dishes.

There was an air of decadence in the opulent room. She wasn't impressed.

"We could continue our conversation more comfortably this evening at my home," he suggested, implying there was more than business on his mind.

She shook her head. "I have an appointment later."

"Nothing so important that it can't wait until tomorrow?"

Thamby was slipping into the city. The man behind the desk wouldn't understand if she told him the truth. Her loyalties were divided between the country of her birth and the land in which she had spent so many years as a child.

"I suggest I present my report to you here," she countered.

He nodded and leaned back in his large upholstered chair.

"Let's get on with it. What have you found out about where Vu is being held?"

She thought she knew. Thamby had to have him in custody in one of the camps in or around the city of Jaffna. The area was under his control.

She knew her superior would be disappointed with what she planned to tell him, but it would protect Thamby and the Tiger movement.

"My sources say he is probably being held by the STF," she replied.

Lal knew Kirbal was lying. The Sri Lankan minister of internal security had a large sum deposited to his Swiss account each month in exchange for confidential information. The source of the funds officially was an Indian businessman in Zurich. But the real source was the RAW funds Lal controlled.

He waited until the woman finished giving her report, then handed her a typewritten financial statement.

The young woman studied the page and became pale.

"You have been followed for the past month, my dear Madi," Lal commented softly. "Every visitor to your apartment has been photographed."

He handed her infrared photographs of Thamby entering and leaving, then passed along another photo—the two of them were naked on her bed.

"These photographs will be forwarded to New Delhi. You will return there within forty-eight hours and keep yourself ready to account for your behavior to our superiors."

"We are supposed to be backing the Tamils. Our own Tamil Nadu State is totally Tamil," she protested.

"Our policies have changed," Lal replied. "We are no longer taking sides."

Kirbal looked at the man sitting across the wide desk. "I suppose you've already reported my indiscretions to New Delhi."

He shook his head. "No. I was hoping we could come to some accommodation that would not force me to let our people back home know what you've been doing."

The woman smiled. "Perhaps it's not too late. Who knows about me locally?"

"There is no report except for these notes. Not yet," he replied, smiling discreetly.

"Then only you and I know about what we've been discussing?"

The young woman was becoming a bore. "Naturally," he said, patronizing her.

"Good." She smiled as she opened her purse.

Lal reached for an ornate silver box on his desk and opened it. He was old-fashioned enough to abhor the way modern young women had become addicted to tobacco.

He admonished her. "Must you smoke?"

"No," she replied.

Surprised at her answer, he looked at the attractive

young woman. In her hands was a modified 9 mm SIG-Sauer pistol with a built-in baffle silencer.

Before the banker could utter a word, she pumped three rounds into his forehead.

The jacketed slugs tore through tissue and bone, carving into his brain cavity.

The white-haired man slumped forward, his blood spattering documents on his once-immaculate desk.

Shoving the weapon back into her purse, Kirbal stood and picked up the typewritten sheet of paper. She was certain no one had noticed her entrance. The staff was used to Lal having a parade of visitors wandering in and out of his office.

When the body was finally discovered, she suspected the blame would fall on government-hired assassins or members of the militant Sikh faction, whose gunmen had been traveling the globe and murdering prominent Indians.

"Now only one of us knows," she told the large, still form as she opened the door and walked down the corridor to the same rear door she had used to enter.

She had to make a call as soon as she could get to a telephone and alert the men.

8

As he peered over the edge of the waterfront warehouse roof, Bolan reflected on his conversation with Hal Brognola prior to embarking on the mission to Sri Lanka.

Their meeting had been brief, and the big Fed had gotten right to the point.

"At the request of the President, John Vu, our former undersecretary of state, had gone to Sri Lanka to attempt to negotiate a truce between the government and the Tamil Tigers.

"It's not just a humanitarian gesture. The United States has been negotiating for years with the Sri Lankan government to lease the former British naval base of Trincomalee as a replacement for our former bases in the Philippines. But the President doesn't want to operate a naval base in a country where the murder of thousands of innocent civilians is a common occurrence. John Vu disappeared three days ago.

"I've found a safehouse for you in Colombo, their main city. An embassy officer, Alden Kendrick, has been summoned back for a month of conferences. You'll be using his place."

As if he read Bolan's mind, he added, "The place is checked regularly for bombs and bugs, and the phone has a built-in scrambler. Use the red Nissan parked behind the building. It belongs to the embassy."

The big Fed handed the Executioner a ring with four keys. "The first two are the main door to the apartment building and the apartment itself. The third is the car key."

Bolan pointed to the fourth key. "What's this open?"

"A side door to the American Embassy in case you need sanctuary in the middle of the night."

"Why would I need that?"

"Striker, the situation in Sri Lanka makes the Somalian and Bosnian carnages seem like snowball fights."

"Do I have a mission name?"

"As long as you're in Sri Lanka, you're Mike Belasko," Brognola replied. "You're a private citizen. I don't have to remind you that if you're caught—by the Sri Lankan government, the Tigers or by the CIA—we'll have to officially deny knowledge of your existence."

The soldier wasn't surprised. Those were the conditions of every mission.

The big Fed handed Bolan a thick envelope. "Everything we know about the country and the key players is in there. Three men control a large part of northern Sri Lanka. Together they run the terrorist group called the Tamil Tigers. We don't have their real names but everyone calls them Thamby, Neelan and Konamalai. Of the three, Thamby is the most powerful and the most dangerous. He treats the other two like aides rather than partners, and he has the biggest following of the trio, and the largest financial backing."

He stopped, then resumed speaking. "The Chinese have a vested interest in keeping the conflict going."

"What's a country like Sri Lanka got that would interest them?"

"Conflict means weapons, and the Chinese are selling every type of weapon and munitions they manufacture to the rebel groups. Our Intel suggests a new shipment is supposed to be arriving in two days. The location of the warehouse where the Chinese will store it is in the envelope.

"One more thing, Striker," he said, handing Bolan a sheet of paper that bore a typed message. "The ambassador in Colombo passed this message along. That's when I got called in."

Bolan read the note aloud. "'Mr. Vu is still alive. Someone will call you and tell you what is wanted in exchange for his release.'"

The note wasn't signed.

The Executioner looked across the desk at his friend.

"Think it's legitimate?"

"This was enclosed in the envelope."

He handed Bolan a color photograph of Vu holding up a recent edition of the *Times of London*.

"I'd say so."

HAL BROGNOLA'S information was, as usual, infallible, Bolan thought as he watched the cranes lifting the heavy wooden crates high above the freighter, then lowering them onto the dock. The big Fed had said the weapons were coming in tonight. After catching some sleep, Bolan had checked out the vessel earlier in the evening.

The freighter was Chinese, as was the crew. Based

on the name of the vessel—the *Mao Tse-tung*—they weren't from Taiwan.

They were pure mainland China. The crates were marked farm implements, and the bill of lading claimed the shipment had originated in Portugal. Bolan knew better. He had opened two of the crates before climbing the metal stairs to the roof.

The dark-haired American, dressed in his blacksuit and with his features masked with combat cosmetics, knew what was being unloaded: automatic weapons, ammunition, grenades, several kinds of missiles and hundreds of barrels of an obsolete version of napalm-like material. The buyers had probably paid more than ten times what the Vietnam surplus was worth, but Bolan knew that, for the most part, legal channels were closed to them. He suspected that the buyers were the Tamil Tigers, looking for weapons for new recruits to the constantly growing secret army they were building.

It took somebody with power and connections to acquire that quantity of arms so fast, then arrange for the cargo to pass unchecked through the various inspections the government required. Only someone with the money to pay off customs inspectors could have put this together.

Thamby's name came immediately to mind. According to Brognola, the Tamil leader had the funds to convince government officials to look the other way.

There were enough weapons and ammunition on the freighter to kill a lot of innocent people, which, Bolan suspected, was the ultimate goal.

The soldier studied the five men in military fatigues who watched stone-faced as the crates disappeared into one of the large vans lined up on the dock. They were whispering to one another in a dialect that Bolan didn't understand.

He mentally reviewed his options.

To attack the ship with missiles would sink it in port and expose its illegal cargo. But innocent Sinhalese dockworkers would be killed. And the crew would probably be able to slip away in the confusion.

He could attempt to eliminate the five Tamils from his current position, then notify the authorities about the cargo. He dismissed the thought. They were trained killers and wouldn't stand still while he picked them off. He was certain the police— at least some of them—were in business with the smugglers.

The cranes began to pull away from the freighter. Workers swarmed over the deck, securing covers and storing equipment. Bolan saw the captain, a bearded Chinese in his fifties, walk down the gangplank and huddle with the plainclothes guards. They were all checking their wristwatches.

Bolan began to feel the muscles tense in his neck, a warning signal. He drew a deep breath, closed his eyes and forced himself to relax.

The soldier opened his eyes. He was ready to proceed.

First he'd rig the trucks with C-4 and set the timers. The next move would be to eliminate the captain, then the bodyguards. The sound of gunfire would terrify the dockworkers. After they scattered, he could launch a LAW 80 missile at the ship's hull, below the waterline.

Then he'd escape, leaving survivors to explain their armed presence to the police when they arrived.

Quickly he slung the LAW and the M-16 over his

shoulder and made his way to the exit door, cautiously
working his way to the side entrance.

Walking between stacks of cargo destined for other
vessels, Bolan hurried to the armament-laden trucks.
He sliced a wedge of the plastic explosive and pressed
it to the undercarriage of the first truck, then inserted
the miniaturized detonator and timer, giving himself
fifteen minutes to complete his mission.

Repeating the same procedure at each of the next
three vehicles, he hid the LAW and the M-16 beside
a stack of crates, than rose to his feet and moved to
the stern of the freighter. The stench of fish and diesel
oil filled his nostrils as he worked his way to the vessel.

As he approached the gangplank, he heard a noise
behind him. Whipping out his silenced Beretta as he
whirled, he saw the Tamil gunman yank an autopistol
from his holster.

"I found him," the guerrilla shouted in clear English. "The intruder we were warned was coming."

The gunner squeezed the trigger, but Bolan fired
first. Three rounds tore through the Tamil's breastbone
and cored into his heart. Without a sound the dead
man slid to the wooden flooring of the dock.

"Hey, Yanu," a voice called out in English, "Did
you get him? The woman on the phone asked."

Woman? The only person who knew his destination
was Madi Kirbal.

Bolan pulled the body behind some crates, then
moved closer to where the others stood. He found an
observation post and set down his equipment.

The voice called out to the dead man again, "Stop
hunting for the American. We need to get out of
here."

Bolan could see the dockworkers scurrying on the deck, and heard the sound of the four men moving toward him.

He headed away from them, toward the ship.

A uniformed ship officer shouted in alarm. He had found the body and called out for the others.

Bolan saw the frightened Chinese captain running up the gangway. The soldier retrieved his M-16 from its hiding place and lowered his eye to the carefully calibrated sight. The captain had reached the doorway. The big American estimated the distance and swept the gangway with a brief burst.

The captain turned his head, looking surprised, then fell from the gangway into the dockside water.

There was shouting from the freighter, then the engines started.

The soldier heard sounds of someone approaching his position. As he grabbed his gear and moved deeper in the shadows, he was confronted by a Tamil guard. A short burst from the M-16 tore the man in two.

The Executioner reached for a new clip when he sensed someone behind him. He threw himself down and rolled behind a stack of crates, the Tamil gunner firing at his retreating form.

Bolan freed a grenade from his combat vest and yanked the pin. He stood, tossed the bomb over the cases, then dropped. Seconds later the explosion blew the Tamil gunner to pieces. Bits of human flesh and bone rained down from above.

The soldier heard the sound of footfalls coming toward him, then the movement stopped. He unleathered the Desert Eagle and held the heavy handgun with both hands, waiting patiently.

The footfalls started again, the stalker moving

slowly, carefully. Bolan turned his head toward the sound. He waited, then abruptly lifted the handgun and squeezed the trigger.

The bulky man who hovered over him, holding a .45 ACP pistol, looked shocked as the bullets tore into him. He stared at Bolan, hate burning in his dying eyes, then fell facedown into a pool of his own blood.

Pulling himself to his feet, Bolan gathered his equipment and hurried to the dock.

The ship was pulling away. He opened the LAW and set the distance. Aiming carefully, he released the HEAT warhead at the ship, which penetrated the rusting metal below the waterline and created a gaping hole.

A series of explosions from inside the hold shook the rusty vessel, telling the Executioner that the missile had detonated the ammunition left in the holds.

The ship began to take on water, settling slowly. Bolan threw the empty LAW tube as close to the vessel as he could. If investigators found it, they would assume it had been part of the cargo.

Then he remembered there were five Tamil guards. He glanced at his wristwatch. He had only five minutes to find the fifth guard and get away before the dock vanished under the impact of the plastic explosives.

Bolan rammed a fresh clip into the Desert Eagle and moved cautiously through the aisles of crates, realizing, when he heard the sound of police sirens, that time was almost up.

He moved around a low stack of crates and spotted the last gunner.

"Throw the gun away and give yourself up. I won't hurt you," the soldier shouted.

Bolan could see the decision process working as he watched the man's facial muscles twitch. The face became hard. He'd made a decision.

The gunner quickly raised his gun. Bolan set his body to withstand the recoil of his huge weapon and started to squeeze the trigger. Then he stopped. The Tamil gunner had rammed the H&K against the side of his head and fired. Bits of gray-white matter sprayed out of the opened skull. The last hardman had preferred to take his own life rather than risk capture.

Glancing at his wristwatch again, Bolan realized only two minutes remained before hell unleashed its fury on the dock.

Bolan raced for the vehicle he'd borrowed from Kirbal, jumped behind the wheel and floored the gas pedal. The Land Rover shuddered at the sudden rush of fuel and sped across the dock and onto the road in seconds.

As he headed toward Colombo, the Executioner felt the earth shake, then heard a gargantuan explosion pummel the air. The sky was lit up with flares and rockets crossing one another, while the exploding ammo created a tumultuous cacophony on the collapsing wooden dock.

The Executioner had spoken in a loud, explosive voice. The Tamils now had to know they had a wolf in the fold.

9

Downtown Colombo resembled a birthday cake. Many buildings had been constructed out of pink sandstone, and victorian arches and white parapets seemed to accent the archaic structures.

The massive Regency-style buildings blended with austere statues of Queen Victoria and other relics of nineteenth-century Ceylon.

Stately Galle Road had served since English rule as a promenade for young people, and tonight was different from no other evening. Slim, smiling women, some wearing traditional saris, others wearing Western clothes, glanced shyly at the young men who waited to ogle them at the street corners.

As he made his way through the streets of Colombo, Bolan reluctantly accepted the reality that Madi Kirbal intended to have him killed.

Bolan had one more place to visit before he confronted the woman: the warehouse where the vans had planned to transport the contraband weapons. He suspected there were more weapons stored there, guns and grenades that would be used to kill many thousands of innocent civilians.

The one-story sandstone structure was located on Old Moor Street, near the Pettah bazaar district.

Bolan pulled the Land Rover to the curb and parked

it. Checking his handguns and the Uzi, he ensured the magazines were full, then set the Uzi on selective fire and shouldered it.

The Israeli-made weapon was a reliable tool. Weighing less than seven and a half pounds, the powerful submachine gun was only seventeen inches long from the tip of its stubby barrel to the end of its folded metal stock. Each magazine clipped into its grip held twenty-five rounds of high-velocity ammo. The weapon could be fired one-handed when necessary.

Nine millimeter parabellum bullets hurtled out of the barrel at the rate of six hundred rounds a minute, with a velocity of 1,250 feet per second. Changing magazines took but seconds.

Bolan was glad he was holding an Uzi now. It was one of the few weapons he trusted in combat.

The building was dark. He tried to peer through the dirt-streaked windows, but the light inside was too dim to see anything clearly.

The soldier decided to try another tactic. He banged on the door with the butt of his Uzi, then stepped to one side and waited.

The door opened, and three Orientals in fatigues looked outside. In a Cantonese dialect, they shouted a question that Bolan didn't understand.

He kept silent.

Two of the guards left the warehouse and looked around.

The Executioner stepped out of the darkness, the silenced Uzi grasped in his right hand. Unleashing a sustained burst from the Israeli subgun, he saw the first guard stare at him in shock for a moment, then crumple in a heap on the ground as life pumped out of his arteries and onto his fatigues.

The second Oriental hardman swung his AK-47 toward Bolan.

In one smooth, fluid move Bolan chopped at his adversary's throat with the hardened edge of his palm. He could hear the small bones in the neck breaking as his palm pushed through them and ruptured the man's carotid blood vessel. The corpse spun, then fell against the side of the warehouse door before sliding slowly into the dirt.

The third guard stepped out to stare at the bodies of his two fallen comrades, then moved into the street to kill the man who had committed this unthinkable act.

He had hesitated too long. The Uzi spit a volley of rounds that destroyed his face before he could lift his AK-47. His lower jaw dissolved as the slugs exploded into fragments inside his mouth. He fell forward and collapsed at Bolan's feet.

The Executioner stopped and listened for any sounds that might indicate that there were more gunmen waiting in ambush inside the building. There was none. Instead the area was filled with an eerie silence. He risked a peek inside.

Except for the tall stacks of crates lined up in rows, there was nothing and no one in the building.

The Executioner wasn't fooled. Attempts to lull him into similar traps had been tried before. The piles of cartons were adequate hiding places for assassins. Any number of armed killers could be waiting for him to pass by.

He moved cautiously as he entered the building, trying to make as little sound as possible. But, even as softly as he moved, he could hear the slight sounds made by the soles of his combat boots.

Bolan stopped short when he heard a shuffling noise above him. Glancing up, he saw two fatigue-clad Orientals, gripping their 7.62 mm Type 85 submachine guns as they climbed over the top of a stack from the other side. Before the soldier could respond, the men had dropped on their stomachs and prepared to fire.

There was no time to aim. Bolan swung up his Uzi and squeezed off six rounds. The shots found their targets, coring the brains of the two would-be snipers.

At the sound of booted feet heading his way, Bolan unclipped a frag grenade from his combat vest, pulled the pin and threw the multigrooved bomb in a slow, loping spin over the tops of the tall stacks.

Flattening against the stone floor, he covered his head with his hands as the grenade exploded into thousands of deadly metal fragments across the room. A series of explosions rocked the stacks of crates, destroying many.

The explosions finally became fewer and fewer, then stopped.

Crouching behind the heavy wood cases, the soldier waited to see how many men would attack.

Nine fatigue-clad men charged him, but the Executioner was ready. He weaved the Uzi back and forth in a tight figure-eight pattern that punched the attackers to the floor.

Only one showed signs of life, moaning as Bolan leaned over him.

"Where is the Indian negotiator being held?" the soldier asked in Cantonese.

In response the hardman made a move toward his auto-pistol. Bolan ended his adversary's desperate attempt to continue with the battle with a pair of slugs that tore through the man's chest and out his back.

Now that the enemy guns had been silenced, there was one more thing Bolan had to do. Digging into his vest pockets, he withdrew slices of C-4 plastique, as well as detonators and timers.

Setting them for five minutes, he plastered the bombs on cases of ammunition and rockets around the large warehouse, then ran out of the building and jumped into the Land Rover.

As he sped around the corner and down another street, he could hear the first of the explosions shatter windows in the area. Pausing momentarily, he looked back.

The sky was filled with flames, bits of wood, sandstone and metal. The impressive display brightened the entire area momentarily, then a cloud of dust began to settle on the streets as the last explosion consumed what was left of the warehouse and the bodies in it.

BOLAN SAT ON THE EDGE of the bed in the Colombo studio apartment that was serving as a safehouse. He had tended a minor wound on his upper arm, which he had sustained during the firefight.

He started to let his eyes close, then forced them open.

There was still Madi Kirbal to contend with. He had phoned her several times, but the calls went unanswered.

She had a lot of explaining to do. If she could.

Bolan picked up the list of people who might not want John Vu to succeed.

The minister of internal security was at the top of the page.

There was nothing Madi Kirbal had written that he didn't already know from Brognola's reports. More than a million dollars American had been transferred to the government official's numbered Swiss account.

At Bolan's suggestion, Brognola had gone through contacts to locate the Swiss bank where the minister kept his payoffs. A little judicious investigation by Aaron Kurtzman's cybernetics team had turned up a wealth of usually confidential information.

The rest of the list was what Bolan had expected— business and minor government officials who provided assistance and confidential information to the various fringe groups trying to stop the Tamils from gaining political power. There were a lot of people on the list who would soon have their day of reckoning.

But there was a glaring omission in the list. Thamby's name was missing. Only the names of his two coconspirators, Neelan and Konamalai, were listed.

Bolan suspected Kirbal was involved with the Tiger chieftain. The woman was obviously more than she pretended to be.

10

Allan Bandaran's Rolls-Royce waited outside the Lanka Oberoi Hotel on Galle Road, in Colombo, a huge man sitting behind the steering wheel on the right side. Formerly a member of the highly professional Keenie Meenie Services, Archie MacDougall had worked as personal aide and bodyguard for the Sri Lankan minister for several years.

The hard-featured blond Englishman kept searching the faces of pedestrians, looking for the person he was supposed to meet. Despite the hot sun and oppressive humidity, the driver wore a starched white shirt, black tie and gray woolen suit.

A smartly dressed Indian woman stepped through the front door of the hotel. Looking around, she saw the limousine and walked to it.

"In the back," the driver said coldly. He wasn't used to driving the woman.

"Why, Archie, you sound so formal," she said mockingly.

"Damn it, Madi," the Englishman behind the wheel growled, "I had to sneak out to meet you. What was so important?"

She got in and closed the door. "I was just in the mood for one of our get-togethers," she purred.

Thamby had ordered her to find out what the minister of internal security knew about the American diplomat.

MacDougall rubbed the scar on his neck. Pointing to it, he growled, "But no more scratches I'll have to explain."

Kirbal said nothing in reply as the long black vehicle sped through the city to her apartment.

She wondered if the American agent had survived last night's waterfront battle, as no one had informed her yet. She was certain that her call had given the men enough warning to set traps for him. Somehow she knew there would be a coded message waiting for her, reporting Belasko's death.

Right now she had something else in mind, such as information the Englishman would carry back to the minister.

"I just heard something I think would please your employer," she commented, leaning on the partition between the front and rear seats of the limousine.

Or cause him to do something in panic, she added silently.

"Even if the American diplomat is killed," she continued, "his government is prepared to send the secretary of state to replace him."

She watched MacDougall try to hide his surprise.

"Is that a fact or rumor?"

She forced herself to smile. "A fact."

She knew the message would be passed along to Allan Bandaran, and the search-and-destroy missions by his storm troopers would end up as headline-stealing victories for Thamby and the Tamil Tigers.

MacDougall HAD REPORTED that Kirbal wanted to meet him before he'd left to pick her up at the hotel.

"Another painful romantic interlude, Archie?" Bandaran asked.

"I don't think Madi Kirbal does anything without some deep motive."

"According to my communications people, Miss Kirbal has been placing and receiving calls from the north of the country. The caller never identifies himself, but it is always the same man. I suspect she plans to continue passing information to him."

"And you want me to make sure she can't."

"Exactly."

"Consider it done, Minister," the blond man promised.

THE TAMIL CHIEFTAIN barged into John Vu's dismal cell.

"Still no word from your government," he shouted. "We feed you and give you shelter while your President makes us wait like slaves for his decision."

The diplomat was stoic. "It isn't my government's decision to make. Dividing Sri Lanka into semiautonomous regions is up to the government and citizens of your country."

"Like everything else, the American government owns Sri Lanka," Thamby snapped angrily. "I have seen—"

The door to the cell suddenly opened, and two heavyset men in fatigues entered.

Thamby looked surprised.

Neelan, the stouter of the two, wore rimless glasses. A purple birthmark covered most of the left half of his face. He controlled the guerrilla bases south and east of the city. Konamalai was tall and thin. His nose seemed more eaglelike than human. His eyes seemed fixed in a permanent steely glare. Konamalai was responsible for the Tiger camps north and west of Jaffna.

Thamby tried to remain stoic, but finally he couldn't contain his curiosity. "Neelan. Konamalai. Why are you here?"

Konamalai signaled Thamby to step outside.

Shutting the door to the barred cell, Konamalai stared at the Tamil chieftain. "You haven't been told?"

"No, what?"

"The ship carrying our supplies has been destroyed."

"An accident in the gulf?"

"An American mercenary planted explosives in the ship," the man replied, cold anger showing in his face.

"At least the Chinese's warehouse has some supplies," Thamby reminded them.

Neelan shook his head. "That, too, was destroyed. By the same American, we believe."

Now Thamby understood the message Madi had left with Lalith, his personal aide, about the American mercenary being more dangerous than she had expected.

He had tried to call her back, to tell her he wouldn't be able to make it into Colombo as arranged. But she hadn't answered her phone.

"Our warehouses are running low on weapons and supplies. If we are going to join in an offensive during the monsoon season, we will need some of what you have in your warehouses," Konamalai said bluntly.

Thamby knew the man wasn't making a request. It was a demand, and Thamby was bothered. It was true that his warehouse was filled. But at the rate of recruiting, it would be empty in a month.

"Can the Chinese rush us more supplies?"

"I contacted him," Neelan replied. "He said it would be at least a month before his government could duplicate our order."

Thamby remembered Atwater. "The English mercenary, Clay Atwater, has been calling about a shipment of weapons and ammunition to which he has access."

Neelan shook his head. "Atwater works for the Sinhalese. Murderers from the special task force would be waiting for our men."

Thamby wasn't convinced. If indeed STF killers were waiting, then Atwater would die. Besides, the problem of getting arms was Neelan's and Konamalai's, not his.

"Perhaps there is another way for you to get weapons and supplies," he suggested.

He led the other two back into the cell.

Thamby pointed to Vu. "This is the man the Americans sent to convince us that they wanted us to be at peace with the government," he said sarcastically.

The negotiator held out his hand. "John Vu, gentlemen."

Neelan ignored the outstretched hand and pointed to the chair. "Sit down, Mr. Vu," he ordered.

Thamby took over from his coleader. "How much are you worth to your government?"

Vu was puzzled by the question. "I don't understand."

"A representative of your government destroyed vital weapons and supplies last night. We hold your government responsible for replacing them."

Neelan took over. "How many carbines, how much ammunition, how many grenades, rocket launchers, rockets and military vehicles will your government send to get you back?'' He paused, then added, ''Alive.''

Thamby could sense Konamalai's disapproving glare. The eagle-beaked man was still filled with some moralistic notions about the purity of the Tiger movement. Noble but unrealistic, the tall Tamil leader knew.

''I wish to talk to this man,'' Konamalai said coldly, ''alone.''

Thamby couldn't stop Konamalai without losing face.

''Talk all you want in this man's cell,'' he said.

The lanky man waited until the other two Tamils left the cell, then asked, ''Why are you here?''

Vu was startled by the man's icy tone. ''I thought you knew,'' the diplomat replied.

''You tell me.''

''The President of the United States sent me to try to work out a truce between you and the government so the killing would stop.''

Konamalai still looked skeptical. ''Why?''

Vu recognized a kindred soul. Even he hadn't believed the Chief Executive until he'd completely leveled with him.

''The British used to have a naval base on the northeast coast of Sri Lanka,'' Vu stated. ''We've been talking about leasing it. But the President doesn't want to put a military installation in a country where internal revolt is going on.''

The gray-haired Tamil stared at the American as he weighed the answer, then nodded. ''That makes sense,'' he said finally.

''But I don't think the President is going to give

you one round of ammunition to get me back. He doesn't operate that way.''

Konamalai made no comment. He studied the American intently, then stood. ''It is time we rejoined the others.''

THAMBY WAITED for Vu to take a chair in his office, then repeated his question. ''How much will your government give to get you back?''

''I don't think they'd give you one gun for me. My government doesn't pay ransom to kidnappers, especially weapons.''

''All governments sell weapons. We do business with quite a few who compete for our money,'' Thamby replied. ''Why is your government any different?''

The American shrugged. ''You can try, but you won't get anywhere bargaining for my life. I volunteered to come over here to try to get you and the government to come to a truce. Nobody sent me.''

''Then we will have to wait and see what your government thinks you're worth.''

Vu had never encountered anyone as cold-blooded as the Tamil confronting him. ''I came here with peaceful intentions,'' he reminded the Tiger chieftain.

''Let us hope that the response from your government will let you leave with them,'' Thamby said, smiling icily. ''Otherwise we will send you back to the United States dead.''

''Perhaps,'' a voice said, amending the statement. Thamby turned to see who had spoken. It was Konamalai.

11

The Boosa Camp consisted of rows of low white-washed buildings surrounded by barbed wire. Hard-faced men in sweat-stained uniforms patrolled the open ditches beyond the electrified fences. It was here that Bolan hoped to get his first lead on where to find Thamby and John Vu.

Garbage filled the almost-empty streets, and a handful of prisoners in filthy prison garb moved aimlessly, pushing large brooms at the piles of filth.

Expressionless armed guards kept staring at the list-less captives from the other side of the barbed wire fence. Bolan studied their faces. All of them wore the callous look of men who had killed too many people to feel emotion any longer.

The Executioner waited until an armed patrol passed, then picked up a rock and threw it at the last of the soldiers marching by.

Falling behind a small rise, he watched as the irritated guard stopped and looked around, then turned back to shout something to the others in the patrol.

The others smiled at one another, clearly knowing what their comrade had in mind, then continued to walk the perimeter of the camp.

Shouldering the AK-47, the guard pulled out a long black club from a belt around his waist and walked back. Slowly he moved along the outside of the barbed wire, searching for where the culprit was hiding.

Combat knife gripped in his right hand, the Executioner waited until the infuriated soldier moved past him, then rose to his feet and wrapped a large, muscular arm around his adversary's neck.

Lashing out with the club, the soldier tried to beat his attacker off, with no success.

Bolan applied just enough pressure to render the man unconscious. However, the sagging body brushed against the barbed wire, generating a cloud of sparks that raced through the soldier, killing him. The electric current held the slain guard fast to the fence.

Bolan heard a loud alarm start to blare. He knew that other guards would race to this spot to see what caused the noise. Moving back into the untrimmed brush, he waited until he heard the sounds of running feet.

As he watched the guards remove the body, Bolan knew the electricity had been temporarily shut off. Removing a pair of wire cutters from a pocket of his combat vest, the Executioner quickly moved to the fence and snipped an opening, then bent the wires toward him.

Knowing how prison guards thought, Bolan was sure they'd believe that there had been an escape. Who in his right mind would want to break into the camp?

Easing through the opening, the big American looked for an avenue of escape.

THE STOCKY STF SERGEANT was stripped to the waist. The teenage girl who stood before him, glaring in defiance, spit out curse after curse. Blood from the torn skin on her back, raw from the continuous beatings from the black leather whip in the noncom's hand, formed into a puddle around her bare feet.

"Butcher! Murderer of innocent children! Unclean offspring of a Colombo whore!"

Raja had been trying for an hour to get the young woman to confess she was the sister of the Tiger chief.

"If I were his sister, he would have already come for me and torn your small genitals from your body with his bare hands!"

The sergeant was stymied. The orders from the colonel were not to kill her, but he said he wanted to find out where Thamby was hiding.

There was one possible solution. He put the whip on a wooden chair and went to the heavy door.

Opening it, he shouted for one of the guards to join him.

A brutish man with scars that covered his face came into the interrogation room. "You called me, Sergeant?"

"Where are your two roommates?"

"Resting in our room. Why?"

Raja untied the young woman and supported her so she wouldn't faint from the beating.

"Here. She's yours. And theirs."

The scarred man's eyes brightened as he threw a huge arm around the teenager's waist. As she began to scream in terror, the sergeant added a warning.

"I want her to be able to tell me about her brother after the three of you are done with her."

The man's mouth curled into a leer of anticipation, then the scarred man started to laugh.

"When we've had our fun, she'll be willing to tell you anything, Sergeant."

BOLAN MOVED SWIFTLY past the one-story buildings, listening for any voices that would give him a clue to who was inside.

Most of the buildings were silent. He had seen the prisoners working in the semibarren fields, trying to till the almost-arid soil.

A woman's scream from two buildings away caught his attention. The voice was filled with terror and hate.

Some instinct told him he had found Thamby's sister. Checking the clip on the Beretta, he headed toward the building.

The windows were blocked by a layer of dust and dirt. Carefully he rubbed away a small circle and looked inside.

A naked young woman was pinned down on a cot. A brutish man was on top of her, trying to force her legs apart, while two uniformed guards watched with lascivious smirks.

Like a cornered wildcat, the young woman slashed at the would-be rapist's face with her nails. Finally, in fury, the heavyset man closed his hand and rammed his fist into her face.

She collapsed, unconscious.

Her attacker spread her legs, then unbuckled his belt.

Bolan tried the doorknob, which was locked.

Flicking the Beretta's fire selector to automatic mode, the Executioner slammed his solid two-hundred-plus pounds against the door, the force of his weight tearing it from its wooden frame.

The man on the bed jumped to his feet and tripped on his pants, which had slipped to his ankles. The other two hardmen recovered quickly from the surprise entrance and grabbed for their assault rifles, hanging from wooden pegs on a nearby wall.

The Executioner stopped them cold with a short burst.

Staring at the huge cavern in his stomach, the first of the pair started to protest, then fell across a second bed in the room. His companion seemed oblivious to his wounds and continued to move toward his assault rifle.

Bolan took out the dying guard with a round that cored his brain.

The brutelike man tried to crawl under the bed, a Chinese copy of a 9 mm Makarov pistol falling from his pants pocket.

The young woman reached down and grabbed it, pointing the weapon at his crotch. A lead slug, embedded with steel shot, ripped into the would-be rapist's testicles, stunning him.

Shocked, he looked down and saw the blood running down his legs. Despite the pain, he forced up the hand that held the pistol, intending to kill her.

Bolan slammed the butt of the Beretta against the enraged man's head. The guard released his grip on the pistol and fell back to the floor.

The Executioner looked at the young woman. "Are you okay?"

When she didn't answer, he repeated the question.

She turned away, still not speaking.

"I'll get you back to your family," Bolan promised.

She shook her head. "No, they are all here. Dead."

"Don't you have a brother who can take care of you?"

"You came to have me betray my brother," she

said, her voice filled with emptiness, then reached for the necklace she wore.

Before the Executioner could stop her, the young woman pulled the ornate chain to her mouth and bit down on it.

Bolan rammed his finger into her mouth. He could smell the almonds on her breath.

Cyanide.

She went limp in his arms. Gently he placed her on the bed and covered her body with a sheet.

THE BARREL-CHESTED camp sergeant wondered how his men were making out trying to get the Tamil women to talk. As he marched down the dirt street to their quarters, he kept slapping his short, leather-covered riding crop against the sides of the building.

"We are not animals," the government official had warned. The words still irritated Raja. The animals were the Tamils, especially those with relatives in the Tiger terrorist movement.

The sergeant wanted no more interruptions. He was busy preparing for the Third Corps War Shu competition, which was coming up in a week. For the past five years, he had been the champion, but young men, with more stamina, were entering the contest. Fortunately none of them had his experience or skills. Many members of the Third Corps had been discharged with permanent physical damage after they had fought him in the past. Raja anticipated that the following week's competition would be no different.

His thoughts stopped when he saw a large man who looked English, or at least foreign. What was he doing in the Boosa Camp?

The overmuscled noncom moved into the shadows

of one of the whitewashed buildings and waited for the foreigner to walk past him. Grabbing the man around his waist, Raja wrapped his other arm around the man's throat and began to squeeze.

Struggling to break free of the strangulation grip, the Executioner suddenly let his body go limp.

The prison guard wondered if he had broken the stranger's neck, and he began to release his hold.

For Bolan the momentary diversion was enough. Reaching behind him with a leg hook, he threw the Sinhalese off balance and followed with an over-the-shoulder throw.

For a heavy man the sergeant was surprisingly fast. Jumping to his feet, he reached out his right leg, hoping to throw the intruder off balance. But before his leg could make contact, the big foreigner moved backward in a dancing motion.

Exploding with fury, Raja threw himself at the stranger, concentrating his anger into his two massive arms. Finesse was no longer important. All that mattered was winning.

Bolan started to pivot away, then let his body go limp as the massive man lifted him into the air with both hands, spun him and threw him to the ground.

Slowly he got up. The sweating guard was standing a few feet back, waiting for him to move, his face still flushed with anger.

"You will die from my hands, foreigner," Raja snarled.

"Let's see if you can fight as well as you can talk."

The sergeant recognized the accent. American. This wasn't the time to wonder why this man was here. He could find that out after he had killed him.

The prison guard watched the American, then he

suddenly hurtled his body at him before the foreigner could get his arms up again. For a moment the sergeant wondered if he'd been drawn into a sucker move as the American lightly jabbed his hand at Raja's heart cavity.

It was too late to worry about it. Besides, he had hardly felt the blow. He forced his leg behind the intruder's right knee, twisted his arm and threw him to the ground.

The American lay there, seemingly unable to rise. He held up a hand in surrender.

The prison guard decided to make the American's death painful. Twisting his left foot, he aimed the metal-tipped toe at the center of the fallen man's ear. He knew the pain would be more than the American could tolerate. Afterward he'd crush the windpipe by grinding the heel of his heavy boot into his adversary's throat.

As he pulled his foot back for the final blow, the sergeant felt suddenly weak. It made no sense. The fallen American had hardly touched him.

As he again tried to thrust the toe of his boot forward, he felt the weakness again.

Then he felt nothing as he fell forward to the ground. Bolan's kung-fu heart thrust had killed him.

12

The administration building sat at one end of the camp, next to a pair of wire gates. A parking lot filled with a variety of military vehicles was next to it.

There was a locked door at one end of the building, protected by a pair of dozing uniformed guards.

Bolan suspected it was the camp armory. If he was going to complete his plans for the camp, he needed more firepower than the Beretta and the Desert Eagle.

Edging his way around the large building, the Executioner reached down and picked up some pebbles, then threw them against a wall of the secured room.

One of the guards snapped his eyes open. "What was that noise?"

The other shook his head. "I don't know. Check it out."

"Why me?"

"Because I said so," the other snapped. "And I'm in charge of guarding the storeroom."

Looking disgusted, the annoyed soldier tucked his AK-47 under his arm and walked slowly around the corner.

Bolan was waiting for him, his combat knife in hand. Before the guard could shout a warning, the Executioner tightened his hold on the man's neck and severed the carotid artery. Easing the dead man to the ground, he waited patiently for the second guard.

A voice from around the corner asked a question angrily.

The second guard strode around the side of the building, then spotted Bolan. He raised his AK-47 and started to shout.

The big American dropped him with a couple of 9 mm stingers.

Bolan pulled both bodies against the wall, where they wouldn't easily be seen from a distance. Searching their pockets, he found a ring of keys. One of them, he knew, would open the storeroom of guns and munitions.

AS SMALL AS THE ROOM WAS, it was crowded with a variety of rifles and handguns. Cases of ammunition were stacked in tall piles against a wall. Searching, the Executioner found a case of dynamite. It had most likely been used to blast large boulders during the construction of the road he had seen just outside the camp fence.

A small crate of detonators and fuses was next to the explosives.

Working quickly, the Executioner spread the sticks of dynamite around the room and fitted them with fuses. Attaching the explosive to a long wire, he ran the plastic-covered detonation cord to the front door and wired it to a detonator.

A case of grenades caught his eye, as did a weapon he hadn't expected to find here: an MM-1 multiple grenade launcher. Bolan picked it up and checked it. Someone had loaded the weapon with both fragmentation and incendiary grenades. The next round was a fragmentation grenade.

Resting the cumbersome weapon on a shoulder, Bolan left the armory and searched the area for a discreet way into the large headquarters building.

A window provided him with a possible entrance. Crouching below it, he raised his head and looked inside. It was a large office, expensively furnished.

Behind the desk was a short, cold-faced man dressed in a colonel's uniform. The Executioner knew that this had to be the man who had given the dead noncom his orders.

Smashing the window with the butt of his Beretta, Bolan saw the man turn in his direction then grab for a handgun resting in a belt holster.

Before the colonel could yank it free, Bolan launched the 40 mm frag grenade.

Throwing himself on the ground, the Executioner felt the walls behind him shake as if an earthquake had hit. The window shattered, and bits of flesh and blood showered the broken glass on the ground.

Racing back to the armory door, Bolan set the timer and raced for the gates. Three shots from his .44-caliber Desert Eagle ruptured the lock that held them closed. As he pushed the gates open and sprinted through them, he heard a barrage of rounds being fired in his direction.

Stopping, he turned and saw a dozen soldiers rushing toward him. He raised the launcher and unleashed a pair of frag grenades at his attackers, then threw himself into a right-handed roll, away from the gates.

Bodies and weapons shattered. The opposition was decimated.

The big American checked the launcher. Nine grenades remained.

Aiming the MM-1 in the air, he emptied five missiles at the roof of the administration building, then turned and released the remaining four at the parked vehicles.

An empty sentry box offered the Executioner temporary sanctuary from the hurtling bits of metal and exploding gas tanks. In the distance the roof of the armory lifted five feet in the air as the explosives detonated the supplies inside.

Waiting for the explosions to ease, Bolan dropped the launcher and retrieved his Beretta from its shoulder rig.

More troops would pursue him. It was time to make a run for Madi Kirbal's Land Rover and head toward Colombo.

THE APARTMENT COMPLEX where Madi Kirbal lived was in one of the better neighborhoods of Colombo.

Bolan pulled the Land Rover into one of the spaces marked Visitor. The building looked too expensive for a government employee's salary. Perhaps the Indian government had given her a housing allowance, or perhaps someone else was helping to finance the rent.

Knocking on the front door did no good. There was no answer. Bolan tried the handle, but the door was locked.

Perhaps she'd spent the night someplace else.

He moved around to the side of the building. The patio sliding door was locked, and the draperies inside were closed. When Bolan reached the far end of the building, he knocked on what he thought were her bedroom windows. There was no response.

The bathroom and kitchen windows were at the rear of the building. The Executioner examined them, spotting a slight space between the bathroom window and the groove in which it rested. He worked his fingers into the space, and finally there was enough space for him to slide his hand in. The window rose easily.

Inside there was a strong, unpleasant odor that was familiar. Cautiously he stepped through the doorway and into the living room.

Madi Kirbal lay on her side on the pure white rug, dead. Somebody had stabbed her.

There was a bowl of fresh fruit on the low coffee table and a small pile of napkins. Kirbal had been the perfect hostess to some visitor. A large ashtray on the table had the remains of a sliced custard apple. Someone had used a sharp knife to slice the pear, and to stab her in the chest. It wasn't hard to figure that out. The knife protruded from the small of her back.

It was possible that Kirbal's killer was still in the apartment.

Bolan strode into the bedroom. The bed covers had been dragged onto the floor; drawers were pulled out and thrown on the floor. Someone was looking for something. The soldier wondered if the killer had found it.

There was nothing Bolan could find in the bedroom that gave him any hint of who the visitor had been.

The rest of the apartment had been aggressively searched but was equally barren of anything that remotely resembled a clue.

Whatever had happened here the previous night couldn't have disturbed the neighbors, he decided. Nobody had called the police.

Suddenly he heard an irritating sound, like nails running across a mirror, coming from the bathroom.

Easing the Beretta 93-R from its holster, he moved to the door and glanced inside.

A burly blond man stood in the bathtub, trying to ease the window open. Bolan noticed the parallel scratches around his neck—Kirbal's nails trying to fight the man off, he suspected, as she struggled for her life.

"Hold it," Bolan ordered.

The man started to turn.

"Slowly. Keep your hands where I can see them."

The blond man faced him, and Bolan could see the scratches across his face.

"She tried to defend herself, didn't she?"

"No, she always does this when we're in bed," the man replied in a cockney accent. "Madi's the violent type. Treats lovemaking like a combat exercise."

"Too bad she's dead."

The blond man shook his head. "When we were done, I realized she was dead. Then you showed up. I didn't know if you were another lover or just a burglar."

"We'll let the police sort this out," Bolan replied.

"I am the police. Archie MacDougall," the blond man told him. "At least, I work for the minister of internal security, and he runs the police."

Bolan suspected her murder had less to do with lovemaking and more to do with his mission. But what?

He signaled his prisoner to walk ahead of him into the living room. "Let's call your boss and tell him what happened."

As they moved in the larger room, MacDougall

seemed to fall apart at the sight of the dead woman. With a sudden cry he dropped to the floor next to her body.

"I'm sorry, Madi. We were just playing."

Bolan felt no sympathy for the man. Kirbal was dead. It was up to the Sri Lankan authorities to decide if it was accidental or deliberate.

"Come on, let's get the police here and Madi Kirbal shipped back to her family," Bolan said coldly.

MacDougall turned and stared up at Bolan, then swung his right hand in a slashing motion at the soldier's midsection. Clenched in his hand was the knife that had killed the Indian woman.

Bolan jumped back, seeing the edge of the blade miss his stomach by a fraction of an inch.

Instinctively the Executioner squeezed the trigger of the Beretta, firing a pair of slugs into MacDougall's massive chest. Neither shot seemed to have any effect on the Englishman. He jumped to his feet and threw himself at Bolan, knife raised to plunge into his adversary's body.

Bolan raised the Beretta slightly and pulled the trigger repeatedly. The slugs tore into the blond man's face and neck. He dropped the knife, collapsing to the floor in a heap.

The big American searched the dead man's pockets, one of which contained some folded pages. They were handwritten letters to Madi Kirbal from someone called Rajiv.

The soldier scanned them. Love letters. Bolan could only read the ones written in English. They were filled with promises of what their life would be like when the independent nation of Eelam became a reality.

In another pocket Bolan found a formal-looking invitation to Allan Bandaran's upcoming birthday party. He pocketed the card, curious as to why Kirbal would have been on Bandaran's guest list.

He decided to let the police sort out the bodies in the living room, then let himself out of the apartment.

He hesitated at the Land Rover, deciding to leave it.

As he walked toward the busy corner ahead to hail a taxicab, he knew there were a lot of questions that would never be answered. Not by the Indian woman.

But if she had been the one who called the Tamil guards at the dock and alerted them, it was the last time she would betray anyone.

13

Clay Atwater, former training officer with Keenie Meenie Services, was surprised at the appearance of the minister. People like Allan Bandaran rarely visited his small office, especially unaccompanied.

He pulled up a chair to his small, chipped desk and, in as upper-class an English accent as he could muster, asked, "Is something wrong, Mr. Minister?"

The short, balding man lowered his body into the chair.

"Perhaps. Or perhaps an opportunity for you to add to your personal wealth."

Atwater snapped to attention. He had never known the security official to mouth empty statements.

"What do you know about a missing American diplomat?"

Atwater weighed the value of telling the truth or lying. This was the first time since he'd gone private where he decided it might pay off.

"I've heard that some diplomat came here to try to work out a truce between your government and the Tigers," the former military trainer admitted.

"Did you know the Americans have sent somebody to find him?"

Atwater wanted to smile, but forced himself to look

thoughtful. "I heard words to that effect. A CIA agent, I understand."

"We're not sure. His name is Michael Belasko, and he did not come in through the normal customs channels."

"Do you have a photograph of him?"

"Not a very good one, I'm afraid. It was taken in early evening without a flash."

The smuggler who had sold it to one of the STF agents had taken it while crossing the Palk Strait from India without the American's knowledge.

Bandaran handed the snapshot to Atwater.

The features were difficult to make out. What he saw was a very large, muscular man, with no expression on his face. Belasko was a professional, perhaps an assassin. He had that cold look of professionals.

"Any idea what kind of weapons he's carrying?"

Bandaran shook his head.

Atwater saw an opportunity to add to his almost-depleted bank account. "It may cost a great deal to convince someone to take on so risky an assignment," he commented, testing Bandaran for some clue about how much he was willing to pay.

"How much?"

The free-lancer grabbed a convenient figure. "Forty thousand dollars American."

"Thirty," the cabinet minister countered.

"Make it thirty-five, and I'll find the right man."

Bandaran pushed himself to his feet. "Done."

"I'll need at least half in advance."

The minister walked to the door, then stopped and turned back. "Will you be here around six this evening?"

Atwater nodded. "I'll make it my business."

"I will have a large envelope delivered to you. And if you're successful, I may have an even bigger assignment for you."

The internal security minister hadn't yet decided who had to be next, the American diplomat or the Sri Lankan president. Both had to go if he was to continue receiving monetary gifts.

ATWATER SAT DOWN in the chair behind his desk and locked his hands behind his head.

Getting rid of the agent would be difficult but not impossible.

He had the perfect man in mind for the job, Fernando DaSilva, and the perfect incentive, money. The mercenary was in desperate need of it.

And he just remembered how he could make more of the funds he needed to keep the Macao casino collectors satisfied.

He lifted the phone and placed a call, then replaced the receiver. Once the caller got the message, Atwater was certain he would call back.

BOLAN PLACED an overseas call and asked the operator to phone him back when she reached his party. The number in the U.S. he'd given her was the first of a series of intercepts that would find its way to wherever Hal Brognola was.

Ten minutes later the phone rang. The Executioner lifted the phone and activated the portable scrambler device.

"Striker?"

He recognized Brognola's voice.

"Here."

"How's it going?"

"Not good yet. The contact turned out to be a triple. She was working for the Tamil Tigers, as well as the Indian government and us. She's dead."

"Damn. Was that the only way?"

"The minister of internal security's bodyguard stabbed her. I took him out."

There was a moment of silence, then the big Fed asked, "What do you need from me?"

"I need replacements for my carryall and some hint of where Vu is being kept."

"Okay on the first. Look in the trunk tomorrow morning. Nix on the second request. We know even less than you do. But I'm hoping to meet with some people who may have information."

Bolan wasn't surprised. Whoever was holding Vu wasn't contacting anyone for ransom, and his only possible source was dead.

The soldier was frustrated. Vu was still missing, possibly dead.

He could confront the minister of internal security, but officially Mike Belasko had never entered Sri Lanka.

Bolan remembered the name of the Chinese importer. Chen. Kirbal had mentioned that he imported electronic components and traveled through Sri Lanka to sell them. It was a slim thread, but it was the only one he had at the moment.

CLAY ATWATER RESTED his head in his hands and felt sorry for himself. It had been so easy to make money when he was part of the British Special Air Service, before he got thrown out of the commando unit.

There was always somebody who would pay for information—an Arab, a South African, some IRA big shot who wanted to know where and when the SAS was planning to hit Northern Ireland.

Even when the KMS gave him a job training Sri Lankan police officers, the money kept being thrust on him. Someone with one of the Tamil rebel groups needed information on when the special task force teams would try to attack them. The minister of internal security gave him money each month to keep him personally informed whenever Atwater was contacted by the Tamils.

Everything had gone to hell in the past six months. The Keenie Meenie Services leader had fired him when he found out about the side income, and almost nobody seemed to care about any information he might have.

The money from the minister wasn't enough to cover his monthly expenses and the gambling debts.

But there was another possible source of funds.

The phone rang. Atwater was sure it was the source calling back. He picked up the receiver. It was important that he sound calm and confident.

"I heard that your supplies were destroyed last night. I may be able to provide you with replacements. For a price," he told the person on the other end of the line.

He listened for a few minutes, then replied, "I'll be in my office until after midnight."

RAJIV THAMBY SAT BACK in his chair and stared without expression at the former KMS trainer.

Clay Atwater found that the thick, damp air made it difficult for him to concentrate on the negotiations.

"We can get you a thousand of the latest M-16 carbines and at least twenty thousand rounds of high-powered 5.56 mm ammo,'' he repeated. ''In addition we can supply you with the Americans' best grenades and newest grenade launchers.

''It cost a lot to get my hands on them. Smuggling them into Sri Lanka won't be a breeze. The government keeps a careful eye on what comes into the country. Even more so since your people decided to go on a killing rampage,'' he reminded the Tamil.

''A political necessity, Mr. Atwater,'' Thamby replied calmly. ''Just so nobody would forget we mean to get our own independent country, even if it means killing every Sinhalese to accomplish that goal.''

The mercenary knew an arms merchant from Macao who'd been trying to unload the stolen shipment of U.S. weapons for weeks. The American sergeant and two privates responsible for the theft in Korea had been arrested by the military police. The arms dealer needed to sell the arms and go into hiding before the American revealed his identity and location.

Atwater had been promised a healthy fee for unloading the arms cargo to the Tamils. He could almost taste the money now.

The Tamil threw cold water on part of his fantasy.

''We might not need your weapons if the American can be made to cooperate.''

''Don't count on it. The Sinhalese aren't about to budge on their demands that you surrender unconditionally.''

''The Americans have sent a negotiator to arrange a truce.''

''Other countries have tried to do the same thing,'' Atwater reminded him. ''They never seem to hold water after the press leaves.''

''This time we are holding private conversations

with the American so he knows how far we are willing to go," the Tamil replied, sounding certain of the success of the talks.

"Where are these talks taking place?"

"Where nobody can find him, until we're ready to send him to the Sinhalese."

Atwater drummed the table with his fingertips. "What about the arms?"

"They will have to wait until we know how the American government responds."

He started to get up from the table.

"You know the Americans have sent a specialist to rescue him?"

The Tamil sat down and stared icily at the former KMS staffer.

"So I've heard," he replied in a flat tone.

His own love was in a morgue, awaiting shipment back to India, because of the American agent. At least he was partly to blame. Madi wouldn't have had to put herself in danger if this Michael Belasko hadn't come here.

"I think I can get rid of him permanently."

"Good." Thamby knew how Atwater thought. "How much?"

"What is he worth dead to you?"

"We are a poor people. I could possibly raise five thousand American dollars to defray your expenses."

Atwater suspected he could only push the Tiger leader a little higher.

"I'll have high expenses. Could you make it ten?"

Thamby pushed back the chair and stood. "Done. I will have the money delivered to you tonight. But I will expect immediate results."

Atwater heard the unspoken threat in the Tiger leader's last statement. Deliver or die.

"About the cargo," he added casually. "There are others who want to buy it."

Thamby sighed. "How soon could you deliver?"

Atwater knew exactly where the merchant's freighter was.

"Four hours after I send my partner the money, we can have the arms waiting on the Jaffna docks."

"If only the price was more reasonable," the Tamil commented.

The ex-KMS officer quickly calculated how much less the dealer would take to unload the shipment. He quoted a price.

"Done," Thamby said. "The money for the arms will be delivered with the other money."

"I'll contact my partner. Your men can start getting ready to back up their trucks on the Jaffna docks."

After Thamby left, the suddenly rich Englishman leaned back in his chair and relished his good fortune, then remembered he needed to get the assignment moving. He didn't need a cadre of terrorists hunting for his scalp.

A quick call to an intermediary in the Thai embassy started the message going to the merchant to move the freighter into the Jaffna harbor, then Atwater concentrated on the best way to get rid of the American CIA agent.

He wondered how much he would have to pay the hit man. Knowing how desperate DaSilva was, maybe four or five thousand American, if the man insisted.

Which left more than fifty thousand for him to square his debts in Macao and buy a one-way ticket back to England.

Atwater lifted the phone and dialed a local number. Waiting until someone answered, he tapped the table nervously.

FERNANDO DASILVA COULD trace half his family tree back to the Portuguese adventurers who ran Sri Lanka for many years before the Dutch took control. The other half was pure Sri Lankan.

He had fallen between the cracks when the Sinhalese and the Tamils started killing each other. There were no jobs for anyone who wasn't part of either of the two ethnic groups.

Especially someone whose only skills were those he had developed as a mercenary in Vietnam.

Nobody wanted to hire a professional assassin, not when the STF and the Tigers were involved in wholesale carnage. He had made a decision to try peddling his skills in some other country, perhaps to the Sikhs in the Punjab sector of India. They were always looking to have someone assassinated.

There was one problem. It took money to get to that part of India.

Atwater's call seemed like the miracle he had needed.

Three thousand dollars to find and kill some American. An easy job. Some extra hands would make the job easier, and he knew he could hire as many as he wanted from the street for a hundred dollars each.

He should be able to finish the job in a few days, then pack his sparse belongings and get out of Sri Lanka.

Atwater had provided him with a suggestion.

"He's probably using a safehouse in Colombo. Find

out if any of the Americans have flown back to the United States recently, then check their flat.''

''I'll get started right away.''

''Good. Stop by my office. I have a rather fuzzy photograph of the American agent.''

The phone clicked on the other end.

DaSilva was pleased. Now he had the funds to leave Sri Lanka, or would have in a few days.

Reaching under his bed, he pulled out a shabby leather suitcase and opened it.

Inside was a .45 ACP Colt Government Model pistol, a memento from someone he'd had to kill, and five filled clips for the weapon. Next to it was a 9 mm Skorpion submachine gun. Slipping the two weapons into a cheap gym bag, he left the hotel room.

There were men to recruit, weapons and wheels to be rented and an American to be found and killed.

BOLAN WAS IN THE SHOWER when he heard a dull banging on the front door. Grabbing a towel and wrapping it around his waist, he walked out of the bathroom, leaned across the bed and eased the Beretta 93-R from its holster.

The banging continued.

Standing to one side of the door, Bolan called out, ''Who is it?''

A woman's voice replied, ''I have an envelope for you.''

''You must have the wrong apartment.''

''Not if you're Mr. Michael Belasko.''

The soldier weighed the possibility that the voice belonged to an embassy messenger. There was only one way to find out.

''Just wait a minute,'' he told her, then slipped into

his pants and shirt. Grabbing the silenced Uzi and tucking it under his left arm, he moved to the door.

Quickly he unlatched the door, then moved to one side. The Beretta 93-R was firmly clenched in his right hand.

"Come in," he said.

The door opened and a young woman stepped inside. She looked around, then saw the armed American standing behind her. She stepped back in shock.

"Who are you?"

For a moment the woman said nothing.

"I was ordered to deliver this to you in person, Mr. Belasko," she answered nervously.

"By whom?"

"I handle confidential faxes at the American Embassy. The cover message said not to turn over the delivery to any of the intelligence officers on the staff, but to deliver it personally."

Bolan was still suspicious. "How did you know where to find me?"

"The cover message said you were using Mr. Kendrick's apartment while he was away," she replied.

Cautiously poking his head out of the door, Bolan could see no one waiting. The Executioner slung the Uzi and held out his left hand. She handed him the envelope.

"Sit there," Bolan said, pointing to a small upholstered chair.

The woman moved backward until she hit the chair with the back of her knees, then lowered herself into it. Her eyes were still focused on the Beretta.

Bolan opened the envelope. The fax was from Brognola, and contained just three sentences:

Some good news. You're not on the CIA's hit parade for the next thirty days. And, Striker, stay hard.

The soldier smiled, dropped the envelope and fax on the bed and turned his attention on the messenger

"What's your name?"

"Chandra Sirindikha."

"A Sri Lankan national?"

"No, I was born in Fresno, California. My family emigrated from here thirty years ago."

"Were they Tamils or Sinhalese?"

"Neither," she said. "My ancestors came to this country from Malay with the early Portuguese explorers."

"Why are you here?"

She misunderstood the question. "I explained that I was ordered to deliver—"

Bolan interrupted. "No, why are you stationed in Colombo?"

She looked embarrassed. "Sorry. I thought you wanted to know..." The embassy employee sensed the man's impatience. "When I graduated from the State Department's training program, I was hoping to be sent to Europe or South America. I'd never been out of the United States. But some assignment officer must have studied my background and decided I would be most useful in Sri Lanka."

"What do you know about the current situation?"

"I don't think I should talk about that."

"I'm asking about John Vu."

"I know. The messages to and from the embassy have been moving in and out at a furious rate." She looked up at Bolan. "Do you think he's still alive?"

Bolan shook his head. "I don't know, but I intend to find out."

"Perhaps I can help you, Mr. Belasko."

He sat on the bed. "How?"

"I overhear things. People treat a communications clerk like a piece of furniture. They never seem to notice my presence.

"There are a number of intelligence specialists attached to the embassy. Several of them have been talking about a man named Thamby. I think they know how to find him."

"Who were the intelligence agents who talked about him?"

"I can give you their names, but it won't do you any good. About two hours after they sent an inquiry to Langley about a Michael Belasko, they received orders to leave Sri Lanka immediately and return to the United States. Right now they are on a nonstop jet to Tokyo, where they will change planes for the States.

"But there is a man in Colombo who the intelligence agents employed to get them confidential information." She dug into the shoulder bag and found a small sheet of paper. "His name is Clay Atwater. He was once with the KMS group when they trained the STF troops. Since then, he has been operating on his own from what I heard. But from what I overheard, he knows where Thamby lives."

She handed the paper to Bolan, who glanced at it. It had Atwater's home and office addresses.

"Any idea what Atwater does for a living?"

"Apparently he will do anything for money. Even kill somebody. At least that's what I believe the intelligence agents hired him to do in the past."

14

Chandra Sirindikha had called Bolan, saying she had more information she thought he could use, and suggested they meet at a small, plainly furnished tearoom around the corner from the embassy.

Several calls had come in, she reported, seeking a Michael Belasko. The caller never left a name or telephone number. The embassy operator told her the same man had called again and asked for one of the just-transferred intelligence agents.

When she told the caller the man had been transferred to another country, he'd asked to speak to his replacement.

"Somebody seems anxious to find you, Mr. Belasko."

"Call me Mike," Bolan replied. "Yeah, that's how it sounds." He thought for a moment. "Tell your operator that the next time the man calls, she should give him Kendrick's address."

The young woman looked shocked.

"Somebody may come and try to kill you."

"Or maybe get killed trying."

Sliding out of the booth, he picked up the check and moved toward the cashier. Seconds later a burst of gunfire shattered the large glass window beside where he had been sitting.

Bolan unleathered the Desert Eagle as he dropped to the floor. Rolling at an angle from the shattered window, he saw two forms spraying steady bursts from their AK-47s as they charged toward the tearoom.

"Under the table," he shouted to the young woman.

She reacted instantly, dropping to the floor.

The staccato bursts echoed through the tearoom. Bolan heard the sole waitress scream as a ricocheting slug drilled into her neck. There was another scream, this time from the cashier. There wasn't time to check if either of them was dead.

Bolan raised the Desert Eagle and squeezed off two shots at the nearest gunner. The first round slammed into the man's face, shoving him backward. The second cored his chest.

Rounding on the second thug, the soldier pulled the trigger three times in rapid succession. The heavyset hardman spun before he could fire the automatic rifle. He fell facedown on the hood of a gray sedan.

Bolan's combat sense flared to life. He threw himself into a shoulder roll and turned as a young man in one of the booths pumped a stream of lead from the 7.62 mm Tokarev pistol in his hand.

The soldier swung the big hand cannon toward the new assailant and fired toward his chin, the punk's face exploding in a shower of bloody tissue.

The second youth had revealed the .45 ACP Colt Government Model pistol he'd hidden under his jacket. He jumped to his feet and stared down at Bolan, fear and hate pouring from his eyes as he began to squeeze the trigger.

"Die, American bastard," he shouted as he sprayed lead at the warrior.

Anticipating the path of the slugs, the Executioner rolled in the opposite direction. The tiles exploded as lead from the powerful handgun drilled into them. There was no time for Bolan to aim. He angled the Desert Eagle toward the thug's chest and fired two shots in rapid succession.

The expression in the would-be killer's face didn't change as the hollowpoints tore through his breastbone and exploded into searing fragments inside.

Gasping from the thick, acrid cloud of burned gunpowder, Bolan struggled to his feet and looked around the demolished room.

Slowly surveying the damage, he saw the waitress slumped across the counter, a jagged hole in the side of her neck and one in her temple. Without having to examine her, he knew she was dead.

Moving carefully around the fallen four attackers, he knelt and felt the artery in their necks. They were dead.

Who were they, Bolan wondered, and what were they after?

His musings were interrupted by the wail of police cars. He helped Sirindikha to her feet. It was time for them to leave.

"I guess he knows how to find me," the Executioner commented as he rushed her outside.

"Is THERE a side entrance to the building?" Bolan asked when they reached the embassy.

"Yes. Follow me."

The young woman led him down an alley, then pulled him across a narrow street.

"It's just ahead," she said, pointing to an ornate metal door set into the huge sandstone structure.

Bolan saw three teenagers loitering near the door. Street punks or hired guns? He wasn't sure. They could be both, he reminded himself. Hit men weren't difficult to find in a country like Sri Lanka, and they didn't command big money.

The tallest of the trio, a large, muscular twenty-year-old, grinned as he danced around Bolan. In broken English he bragged, "How about a boxing match, to impress lady. Take best shot."

Bolan moved closer, then suddenly whirled and faced away from the tall youth. Surprised at the unexpected move, the young man rushed Bolan. As he reached out to grab him, the soldier rammed his foot at the bend behind the youth's knee.

Screaming with pain, the street tough went down on his knee and lashed out.

Bolan stiffened his hand and slammed it into his adversary's collarbone. The snapping sound echoed in the darkness of the street as the other two youths stared in astonishment.

The enraged youth jumped up despite the searing pain in his leg, and threw himself at Bolan. The soldier easily stepped out of his reach, then grabbed his wrist and threw him over his shoulder. The tough crashed on the pavement and was suddenly still.

The two youths rushed at Bolan from different directions.

"No, get the girl," the fallen leader yelled.

Bolan was torn between stopping the teenager who was racing toward the small woman, and the punk who was charging at him with a large knife in his hand.

There was no time to weigh the options. He'd get to her after he'd disarmed the attacker who was almost upon him.

Moving to one side slightly, the soldier let the knife arm start to move past him, then grabbed the wrist and let the teenager's forward motion help him.

He flipped the attacker over his shoulder, then kicked the side of his head. Blood trickled from the fallen youth's mouth.

Bolan waited for the young man to move, but he was unconscious.

The Executioner turned to assist Sirindikha and was surprised to see the third youth lying on the ground, moaning in agony and clutching at his crotch. He tried to grab one of the woman's ankles, but dancing a few inches to one side, she kicked the pointed front edge of her shoe into the fallen youth's ear. Screaming at the sudden pain, he rolled onto his face and started to weep.

Bolan stared at his companion. She didn't appear winded or upset. If anything, she appeared almost serene, as if nothing of consequence had taken place.

"A self-defense class at a community college in Fresno," she explained, straightening her clothes. "I'm glad I didn't forget everything I learned."

DaSilva was sweating profusely.

First the four men he had hired to follow and kill the American were killed in a restaurant bloodbath. He assumed the American agent was responsible. They were supposed to wait outside the building where he was staying and shoot him at the first opportunity.

Now the three youths he'd hired to pick a fight with Belasko had called him from the Colombo General Hospital emergency room. The leader of the trio was supposedly an expert at killing with a blade, which was what DaSilva had hired him to do.

Only he was supposed to make it look like the by-product of a street fight.

Atwater wouldn't be pleased.

He would have to find replacements for the men he'd sent. Fortunately, he reminded himself, he hadn't yet paid them for their services.

Searching desperately through his memory, he remembered a local group of collection specialists who worked for whoever paid them. He skimmed through the yellowed telephone book on his night stand and found the telephone number of his contact. It would reduce the amount he kept for himself, but half of something was better than nothing.

He decided it was time to lead the men personally.

15

DaSilva didn't know why they wanted to kill the man named Michael Belasko, nor did he care. It was their business, not his. All that mattered was that he'd been promised a bonus of an additional five thousand by Atwater if he was successful.

Compared to some of the jobs he'd been given, this one was a breeze, and a lot more profitable.

He shut his thoughts off as he spotted the local men he had hired. There were almost a dozen. Gripping the cheap plastic gym bags that contained the Skorpion SMGs he'd provided, they were trying their best to blend into the crowds that jammed the streets. He had checked their credentials as best he could on such short notice.

It was supposed to look like a terrorist attack, an indiscriminate massacre ordered by the Tamil Tigers or one of the other rebel groups. The assault would kill more than just the American, but the resulting panic and confusion would make it easier for all of them to escape.

Finding the American hadn't been difficult. Several of his men had canvassed the area around the Pettah and learned that a big American had been asking Chinese restaurant owners if they knew where to find a Chinese importer named Chen.

There were several restaurants on Chatham Street, and the American hadn't yet come here to ask his question.

A red Nissan pulled into Chatham Street. Behind the wheel was a large, hard-faced man.

Excitement coursed through DaSilva. It had to be him. Belasko.

The man stood and signaled with a gesture of his hand for the gray Toyota at the curb to start moving, then took a position against the outside wall of a small tourist shop and knelt to open his bag.

STARING INTENTLY at the faces on the streets, the Executioner didn't notice the car that had pulled out and fell in behind him until the Toyota Corolla deliberately rear-ended him.

Bolan started to get out of the car when he spotted an ancient Datsun parked at a nearby curb, with its engine running. He looked at the three men standing next to it, staring at the entrance. A fourth man sat behind the wheel. Bolan recognized them for what they were—professional hit men.

One of them spotted him, then gestured to the others. The soldier turned away. Reaching under his jacket, he unleathered the .44 Desert Eagle and slipped it inside his waistband.

He left his car at the curb and started to stroll toward the men, then burst into a run.

The hardmen standing beside the Datsun were stunned that Bolan would be racing toward them instead of trying to flee. The nearest thug whipped out a Skorpion submachine gun, a compact weapon that could pump out a full 30-round clip of 9 mm parabellum rounds in seconds.

Leaning the weapon on the trunk of the car, he started to squeeze the trigger, spraying hot lead at the fast-moving American.

Yanking the big .44 pistol from his waistband, Bolan stopped and assumed a two-handed gun stance and squeezed off two shots.

The first round punched into the shoulder of a thug with deep facial scars, causing him to spin a half turn. The second slug ricocheted off the metal trim of the rear windshield and slammed into the gunner's face, gouging a crater next to the bridge of his nose. The Skorpion fell to the ground as the man tumbled out of sight.

The other two gunners dropped behind the gray sedan. One gestured for his partner to move to the right while he moved left.

Inside the Datsun the terrified leather-jacketed youth behind the wheel slid down in his seat. He reached to grab the AK-47 assault rifle he had put on the seat next to him. Shaking with fear, he dropped the carbine to the floor, then nervously bent to retrieve it.

The soldier moved to his left and fired at the second man, the hollowpoint chopping into his adversary's side. Screaming with pain, the would-be killer turned and washed the area around the Executioner with a continuous burst of lead.

Even under expert control, the compact weapon wasn't very accurate at distances greater than fifty feet. And in the hands of a wounded man, the bullets ricocheted off the cars, the brick walls and asphalt, slamming indiscriminately into terrified restaurant patrons and passengers in passing cars.

Bolan fired another round at the hit man's chest, shattering his collarbone.

Enraged, the assassin loosed a sustained burst of 9 mm death. Two of the slugs chewed through the Executioner's jacket and shirt, drilling into his Kevlar vest with a brutal force.

The punch of the lead projectiles saved the soldier's life, hurling him to the ground and, for the moment, out of the sight of the hit men.

Winded, Bolan waited until the breath returned to his lungs before leaning down and scooping up his weapon.

Despite the blood that covered his face, Bolan's adversary was still standing, still holding his weapon. Suddenly he collapsed and disappeared from sight.

Keeping his body close to the ground, Bolan carefully worked around the bullet-fractured vehicle.

One of the Sri Lankan hit men wasn't dead. Covered with blood from the lead that had torn into his face and chest, the mercenary waited, then jumped to his feet and exposed the Skorpion. He concentrated his rage on killing the American.

But the Executioner beat him to the pull and pumped out a pair of rounds that chewed through the gunman's flesh and into his heart cavity. The man died before his body slid to the ground.

The driver realized he was now the only one of the group left alive. He panicked and threw the car in reverse, then jammed his foot down on the gas pedal. He rammed the vehicle into a handful of hypnotized patrons who had huddled outside the restaurant entrance to watch the gun battle.

Two women were shoved back into the brick-framed entrance and crushed between the heavy vehicle and thick wooden entrance door. Several others threw themselves to the ground, trying to crawl out of the murderous path of the vehicle.

Filled with terror, the driver braked, then raced forward toward the empty road.

Hunched over the wheel, he spotted the man who stood between him and escape.

At the last possible moment, Bolan jumped to the side, simultaneously pumping two rounds at the driver of the fleeing vehicle.

The ancient sedan smashed into a parked Mercedes 450 SEL, the force of the crash destroying the Datsun. The driver was slumped over the wheel, blood streaming down his face.

Bolan rammed a fresh clip into the Desert Eagle and turned his attention back to the Toyota.

The hardmen near the Japanese import panicked as they heard the gunshots and saw their associates fall to the sidewalk. They'd huddled behind the Toyota, hoping the other hit men would stop the American before he turned his attention their way.

But now there was no choice, and two of the gunners pointed their submachine guns at the soldier, venting their rage with continuous bursts.

Bolan fell into a forward roll and came up near the vehicle, firing, while the slugs from the Chinese-made automatic rifles carved into the ground.

The nearer gunner roared in anger as he felt the burning sensation of the .44 slug cutting a deep groove across his forehead. Turning his weapon on the American, he squeezed the trigger and sprayed the area in front of him with metal-jacketed rounds.

Bolan did a side flip and landed two feet away from where he had been standing. In one smooth motion he raised the Desert Eagle and fired two more slugs at the gunmen, taking out both with head shots.

Momentarily shocked, the last surviving assassin, a stout, balding man, could only stare at the bodies.

Bolan took advantage of the situation to duck behind a nearby British-built Ford, narrowly missing the hail of hot lead unleashed by the hit man when he snapped out of it.

There was no way to reach the Sri Lankan without exposing himself, but it was a risk he would have to take.

Ramming a fresh clip into the Desert Eagle, he jacked a round into the chamber and stood, firing rapidly at his enraged adversary.

The round drilled into the hardman's abdomen, tearing into his pancreas. Bits of bloody tissue and splintered bone exploded onto the ground.

Screaming curses in his accented English, the assassin triggered his weapon, unleashing a wild burst before he collapsed to the ground.

A young woman, dressed in a stylish gray suit, was shoved backward into the crowd and cut in two by the lead burning from the dead man's weapon. The slugs cut through her and into the men and women behind her, who had been shoving their way back into the nearest doorway.

Bolan heard a noise to his right and spotted a tall young man who was vomiting. The pedestrians nearby rushed forward and tore into him, like dogs tearing apart a rag doll.

Turning, he saw an older gray-haired man ramming the muzzle of the Skorpion he held into the back of a terrified Indian woman.

Confusion and terror raced through the street. Panicked men and women grabbed the hands of their families and pushed and shoved their way into open doors to restaurants and shops, trampling anyone who came between them and escape.

Bolan focused his attention on the gunman and his now-hysterical hostage. With constant prodding from the lethal weapon in the small of her back, the weeping woman kept moving toward the big American.

He stood still until the hostage was almost next to him. The gunner then shoved her aside and braced his body as he triggered the Skorpion.

The Executioner had waited until the killer had committed to firing before he took action. With the ease of years of practice, he lunged forward in a shoulder roll. Above him he heard the burst of gunfire and the screams of the woman, then he sprang to his feet behind the hit man.

The cold-eyed killer twisted to face the big American. He tried to loose another sustained burst, but the soldier pumped a .44 round into the surprised man's throat before he could aim the SMG.

Bolan searched the corpse's pockets. In his wallet was his Sri Lankan driver's license—Fernando DaSilva—and a slip of paper: See Clay Atwater for money.

DaSilva had to have been given the contract by Atwater, who was the Executioner's next call.

The soldier got into the borrowed embassy Nissan and sped from the scene of the massacre.

He knew that sooner or later someone would remember to call the police. It was time for him to leave.

16

Clay Atwater's business address turned out to be a shabby two-story building on a side street at the other end of the city. The streets were bordered with small warehouses and factories.

On the street level of Atwater's building was a now-closed Oriental medicines shop. A metal door stood at one end of the building, with nothing painted on it. Bolan tugged at the handle, which opened.

As quietly as he could, he climbed the narrow flight of stairs, illuminated by one dim ceiling light on the second floor.

Five frosted-glass doors lined the corridor. The first four bore names: Gandaya Indian Freight Forwarders, G. D. Medical Supplies, Sri Lanka Travel Bureau. One was painted in Sinhalese, which Bolan couldn't read.

The last door was bare.

There was a light on inside. Bolan reached underneath his jacket and loosened the Beretta 93-R from its snug holster.

The handle turned when he tried it. Bolan eased it open, then waited for some reaction. When there was none, he cautiously entered a shabby reception room. It was dark and empty, except for an old metal desk and a few folding chairs.

The only light came from the inner office, and Bolan peeked inside. Everything was covered with dust, and papers and empty beer cans were strewed everywhere.

A balding, squat man had his head down on the desk. As the soldier moved to his side, he could see blood oozing from a huge wound in the side of his head.

It was Clay Atwater.

The top of the desk was clear, except for the remnants of a miniaturized answering machine, which somebody had torn apart.

He was grasping a scrap of paper in his fingers. From the torn edges, it looked as if somebody had tried to free it from his hand. Bolan looked closely and could make out the scrawled name: John Vu.

Bolan searched through the man's clothes and found a wallet made of cheap cloth. It contained several bills and a driver's license made out to Atwater.

Looking around the room, the Executioner decided that there weren't many places the man could have hidden anything. The only furnishings were the desk, three wooden chairs and a small file cabinet where drawers were empty.

Bolan went behind the desk and pulled open the side drawers, which were just as empty as the file cabinet had been.

The chair in which Atwater sat was on wheels. Bolan didn't have much trouble moving it to one side so he could open the center drawer. Except for a sealed six-pack of microcassettes, there was nothing in it.

A ball of shredded tan recording tape lay on the floor under the desk. Somebody had ripped the tapes out of the answering machine and made sure they couldn't be played.

What had the dead man recorded that somebody wanted badly enough to kill him for?

He heard a car door slam, then moments later footsteps pounding up the stairs echoed all the way into the inner office. Bolan rested his hand on his belt close to where he could grab the Beretta and walked back into the reception area.

A voice called out. The accent was local.

In accented English, the voice shouted, "I shall be right down. I just want to be sure we didn't leave anything behind."

A short, muscular Sri Lankan in a police uniform walked in, saw Bolan standing in the center of the inner doorway and almost dropped the Type 54 pistol he was gripping in his hand.

The policeman stared at him, trying to make out his features in the darkened reception room. "Who the hell are you?"

Bolan started to reach for the Beretta, then realized that gunshots could bring reinforcements. He decided to try to bluff his way out of the building.

From the way the numerous scars on the man's face were twitching, Bolan suspected the man was edgy.

"Mr. Atwater and I were supposed to meet here. I guess he isn't going to show up."

"You a friend of his?"

"No. He was helping me solve a problem I had."

The uniformed man backed away from Bolan toward the inner office door. He kicked it open, then turned back and studied the American. His eyes narrowed. Bolan moved his hand inside his jacket.

"I guess I'll leave him a note, if I can find my pen."

What Bolan was waiting for was some momentary distraction so he could bolt out of the office.

The cop lifted the phone and dialed a number.

"It's Conrad, Commander," he said, in a flat, hard voice. All arrogance vanished from the man and was replaced with respect and fear.

"You can tell the minister we took care of him half an hour ago. I don't care what the man on the wiretap reported. There was no money in the office. We came back here to look for the money again, and I found some American snooping around the office." He paused, listening to the person on the other end.

"Why not right here? What's one more?" He looked annoyed as something was explained. "Okay. We'll take him into the forest."

He slammed down the phone and waved the gun at the soldier. "We have to take a ride and meet somebody."

Bolan knew he'd soon be dead.

There was only one thing to do. Bolan played it straight. "Could I leave you a number to call later and tell them I'm okay?"

The local cop smirked. "Sure."

The Executioner reached into his jacket and moved his hand as if he were searching for a pen.

The Beretta 93-R appeared, as the warrior threw himself across the desk toward the officer.

The startled policeman pounded his entire clip at where Bolan had been standing, only the man was no longer there.

Rolling to his left, Bolan raised his weapon and fired a tri-burst at his adversary, the lead chewing gaping wounds in his chest and neck.

Bolan carefully kicked the handgun away from the dead man. Too many times someone supposedly dead had suddenly come to life, ready to continue the battle.

CHANDRA SIRINDIKHA was waiting outside his door when he returned to the safehouse. She looked worried until she saw him.

"The local news program said there had been a massacre in the Pettah district. I was hoping you weren't involved."

Bolan was surprised to see her, and even more surprised to hear her concern.

"More important, I found this." She handed him several pages and a map. "It was hidden in the desk of one of the intelligence officers who'd been transferred."

Bolan studied the papers. They were a rough draft of a report the agent had been preparing for Langley on the location of a Tiger camp the terrorist group had abandoned.

The soldier looked at the map. Someone had conveniently circled a small wooded area fifty miles north of Colombo.

Bolan wondered if the information was genuine, or planted to draw him to the place. Either way, he had to check it out.

"Thanks. You better get out of here before someone spots you," he told the embassy clerk.

"I'm going with you." There was a hard, no-nonsense edge in her voice. "I know the fastest way to get there. Either I go with you, or I follow you."

Bolan quit arguing. Like it or not, he had a companion.

THERE WAS NO BREEZE, so the rustling sound could only mean that some bird or animal was moving, or, the big American suspected, somebody was waiting for them.

Gripping the M-16, fitted with an M-203 grenade launcher, Bolan crouched behind the thick stand of teak trees. Glancing at the young woman next to him, he could see the fear and confusion in her eyes. He didn't think she knew that she was leading him into an ambush. Someone else had set it up.

There were a lot of possibilities, such as the departed CIA men, but this wasn't the time to worry about who was responsible. The immediate problem was escaping the guerrillas who surrounded them.

One thing he knew for sure: the missing diplomat wasn't being kept nearby. This was a place of death—his, if the terrorists had their way.

Staring into the dark, Bolan made a decision. It was time to flush out the enemy. Weighing his options, he set down the M-16 and searched the canvas bag he'd brought with him.

"Whatever happens, stay hidden," he ordered. "If I'm not back in fifteen minutes, run like hell for the car and get out of here."

While the woman stared at him in confusion, Bolan picked up his weapon, loaded an M-40 grenade and launched the first missile in a high arc to his right. Before it landed, he repeated the action to his left, then straight ahead of him.

The three explosions followed in rapid succession, accompanied by screams of agony from those terrorists riddled with scorching slivers of superheated metal.

The Executioner waited for the assault he knew was inevitable. Terrorists, he knew, were essentially cowards who used darkness and hostages to mask their fears and give them false courage. They couldn't afford to look frightened to their peers.

Setting down the M-16, the soldier replaced it with the 9 mm Uzi, fitted with a 35-round clip of steel-jacketed slugs and listened.

Even the soft felt slippers on the terrorists' feet couldn't completely hide their stealthy movements. The soldier waited until he sensed them close, then stood and hosed the area in front of him with a controlled burst of death bringers.

The screams and cries in the dark attested to the deadly accuracy of his aim. But the sound of footfalls tearing into the forest in the opposite direction let him know there was at least one survivor.

"Wait here," he told the woman with him as he rammed a fresh clip into the Uzi and strode forward.

A dozen bodies were sprawled on the ground, their awkward poses a testament to their sudden deaths.

Bolan heard a noise and whirled, preparing to fire his weapon.

It was the woman.

"I told you to wait."

"No. I led you into this trap, and I had to see the faces of those you killed."

He stepped aside and watched the darkness for any hint of movement, while Sirindikha moved from body to body, studying the faces of each carefully before moving on.

"No, I don't recognize any of them," she said. "They look like..." She hesitated. "Like ordinary people."

Suddenly she gasped as she looked closer at one of the corpses.

"She's a woman," she said, looking shocked.

"They *are* just ordinary people, men and women who've become part of some cause that controls their lives. What the Tigers believe in isn't bad. It's what they do to achieve their goals that needs to be stopped.''

Bolan heard a soft sound, like that of someone moaning. He put a finger to his lips, then pushed her aside and moved to the source.

One of the guerrillas held his hands against his stomach, as if he hoped he could stop his entrails and blood from spilling on the ground. Bolan knelt beside him.

''Who sent you?''

''We were many. You were one. Why are you alive?''

''Where is the American?'' the Executioner asked, knowing from the extent of the man's injuries that he was dying, and that little time remained.

The young man's face filled with confusion.

''American? You are the only American here.''

''The American who came here to bring peace,'' Bolan continued.

A faint expression of understanding flashed across the dying terrorist's features.

''The leaders have said that there will never be peace until we are free,'' he gasped. ''They are trying to convince the man from across the water—''

The young guerrilla stopped talking. Suddenly his eyes looked past Bolan and became glazed with death.

For all the killing that had taken place, the only thing the Executioner had learned was that John Vu was probably still alive.

17

The President had asked Hal Brognola to report on the progress of the rescue mission.

"Nothing concrete to report," the head of Stony Man Farm stated bluntly after taking the chair offered by the Chief Executive.

"Obviously somebody knew he was coming. The kidnapping took place within a day of his arrival."

"Who? Except for my personal secretary, I made sure nobody else knew about my request." He thought for a minute. "Perhaps John mentioned it to someone." Then the Man shook his head. "No, that's not his style. John's an old poker player. Plays everything close to the vest. Do you think some foreign agents tailed him?"

"Maybe we ought to look inside and not outside."

"You think that we've got people in our country who could do something like this, for some personal gain, Hal?"

"I think every country does, Mr. President."

"How do you think I should play the news?"

"If it was up to me, Mr. President, I'd keep a lid on it. Only a select few people—and the kidnappers— know about John Vu's status."

"Is Striker still alive?"

"Yeah, and not happy that he hasn't been able to get a solid lead on Vu's whereabouts."

The President looked somber. "Someone is going to join us who might be of help to Striker. At least I hope he is."

Brognola wondered who the person was. One thing he was sure about—it wouldn't be anyone from the CIA. They'd prefer the Executioner dead.

"My visitor should be here, Hal. Okay if I bring him in?"

"Anything I can give Striker to speed up his search would be greatly appreciated."

The Chief Executive reached for the intercom and pushed a button. Moments later the door opened and a slim, balding man entered the room.

The President looked at both men. "Do you two know each other?"

Brognola recognized the man from prior interagency meetings: Rex Medford, director of State Department Intelligence and Research Services.

Medford crossed to where Brognola was sitting and shook his head. "Good to see you again," he said.

The Chief Executive pointed to an empty chair. "Sit down, Rex."

The State Department official did, and waited for the President to speak.

"Rex's people may be in a position to provide your man with both information and assistance." The President turned to Medford. "Take over, Rex."

"We've been watching the situation in Sri Lanka deteriorate daily. Because we were afraid that CIA might be playing on both sides, we assigned our own people to build up a file of possible contacts."

Brognola immediately liked the balding man for not

pulling punches about the CIA's self-interested meddling.

"One of our sources sent a signal through an intermediary in Madras that he'd heard an American was being held for ransom in a village just outside of Jaffna."

Brognola sounded annoyed when he asked, "Why didn't your people contact the government and have them send troops in to rescue him?"

"The people in charge of such an operation would have made sure the American—especially if it was John Vu—was killed and the blame placed on the Tamils," Medford explained. "Instead we had our man—in this case our woman—keep in touch with our Tamil source for any news about Vu."

"How can she help the man I sent over?"

"First of all she's fluent in the various Sri Lanka languages. And even though this is her first field assignment, she's already proved herself resourceful."

Something clicked in Brognola's head. Striker had mentioned a woman from the embassy.

"The embassy communications clerk?"

Medford nodded. "Chandra Sirindikha. And I believe she's already provided your man with assistance."

The President interrupted. "This Tamil contact, will he cooperate with the man Hal Brognola sent over to rescue John?"

"I believe he will, Mr. President."

The Chief Executive pressed the point. "Are you certain?"

"John Vu was one of ours. I'm positive Father Tomas will do everything he can to help free the former undersecretary of state."

"Send your woman a signal to make the contact," Brognola said.

The President looked at the big Fed questioningly. The Stony Man Farm head nodded. It was risky, but for now it was the only game in town worth playing.

"I only pray that we're not too late," the Chief Executive said, sounding worried.

"On behalf of my man in the field," Brognola replied, "I second the prayer."

THE MINISTER of internal security was venting his rage to the senior commanders of the special task force.

"A simple assignment," he yelled, pacing the length of his large office. "Find the American mercenary and the missing diplomat. Your men can find neither."

General Kumartanga, operations commander of the elite attack troops, looked uncomfortable. "Our usual sources have been unable—or unwilling—to tell us anything." He hesitated, then added, "Clay Atwater would have been more helpful had he lived."

"Is that an accusation?" Allan Bandaran stared at the uniformed officer. "Atwater couldn't find a bag of gold if it were sitting on a table in front of him!"

"If we go along with the theory that the Tigers are holding him captive, we could launch surprise assaults on their bases and rescue him," Colonel Senanayake, one of the senior field commanders, suggested.

Bandaran considered the suggestion. The STF knew the location of most the Tigers' camps, but not all of them. Still, if the Tamil terrorists were attacked, they'd retaliate, probably by killing the American diplomat.

The minister smiled. The Tamils might do what his own forces couldn't.

"Excellent suggestion," he said. "Put it into action immediately."

COLONEL CHEN WAS MET at the airport at Katunayake, twenty miles north of Colombo, by his secretary, May Ling.

The attractive woman grabbed his suitcase and led the way to where she'd parked his Mercedes-Benz.

"Good trip, sir?"

If constant threats, accusations and interrogation by the minister of state security and his aides constituted a good trip, Chen had had one.

"Business trips are always tiring," he replied non-committally.

She placed his small bag in the trunk of the car, then got in behind the wheel.

"Home?"

"Until we find a new warehouse, my home will also serve as my office."

He had a new assignment: to find and kill the American who'd come to rescue the negotiator. His superiors wanted revenge for the valuable supplies the mercenary had destroyed. And until Chen did, he would be under a cloud of suspicion in Beijing. It was imperative he start the search immediately.

"You will have to work later tonight. There are plans to be made."

"Regarding the diplomat?"

"No, he is next. We must find the American who destroyed the valuable property that belonged to the Chinese people," Chen said coldly.

"This might interest you, Colonel," May Ling said, handing the gray-haired intelligence officer a sheet of paper.

Chen studied the document. "Where did you get this?"

"One of our comrades works as a cleaning lady at the American Embassy. In going through the files, she found that one of the officials was away on official business, but that his apartment was being used by somebody else."

"The American, Mike Belasko!" Chen sounded triumphant. "Now we can eliminate this enemy of the people."

"When?"

"Tonight. Call our people and tell them we must meet." He shook his head. "This time I will lead them to make sure the task is successfully completed."

TWELVE MEN WERE deployed at the front and back of the building where Chen believed the American was hiding. He had gathered a truck and van to carry the men and their weapons discreetly to the area.

Now the van filled with five men waited in the rear, while the truck and seven heavily armed professionals sat at the curb in front.

Chen and May Ling waited in his Mercedes-Benz 500.

The American mercenary had to leave the building some time. Lights were on in the borrowed apartment, but they had been waiting an hour and he hadn't come out yet.

The Chinese colonel gestured for the driver of the truck to join him.

When the Sri Lankan professional did, Chen ordered, "Send somebody in to start a small fire outside his door."

18

Bolan had just finished cleaning his guns when he smelled smoke from the hallway. Grabbing the Desert Eagle, he loaded a fresh clip, then cautiously opened the door.

The corridor was empty, and there was more smoke than flames. Someone had spilled flammable liquid on the hall carpeting and set it afire. Deliberately, the warrior suspected, but he didn't know who.

Grabbing some blankets from the bed, he threw them out into the hallway and smothered the fire. Then he gathered the rest of his weapons and loaded them. The Beretta's leather went on his left shoulder, while the rigid holster for the Desert Eagle was slipped onto the thick belt that snaked through his waistband loops.

Shrugging into the combat vest, heavy with magazine replacements and grenades, the soldier grabbed the sheathed combat blade and strapped it to his forearm.

Starting a fire was an old trick to flush out the enemy. He needed to know who was waiting for him to come out.

Digging into his carryall, he found his Zeiss binoculars and slung the powerful opticals around his neck.

He started to leave the apartment, then decided to

call the local fire department. The confusion of their arrival would help him make his escape.

He picked up the canvas carryall in his left hand, then slipped out of the apartment and made his way to the roof, where he had a clear view of the ground below. As he studied the street in front, he saw a truck and a Mercedes-Benz parked at the curb, two vehicles he had never seen on the quiet side street before.

Even using the binoculars, it was hard to make out faces, but the couple in the Mercedes looked Oriental.

Moving across the roof, he looked down and saw a van, with several men standing next to it. All of them were Chinese.

He smiled coldly. Colonel Chen was coming for payment on the inventory he'd lost.

His own car, the red Nissan, was parked at the opposite end of the rear parking lot. Obviously none of the men knew it was his. No one seemed to be paying attention to it.

It was a safe bet that they were all armed and trained, and there was no point in waiting until they brought the war to him. He would have to take the initiative if he was going to survive.

The door to the roof suddenly opened, and a head popped out and looked around.

Chandra Sirindikha.

When she saw Bolan, she sighed in relief.

"You weren't in your apartment. When I saw all the smoke I thought you'd been shot. But I took a chance and came up here to look for you." The young woman was holding a 9 mm Heckler & Koch P9S autoloader.

"I didn't think communications clerks carried guns," he stated.

"When I couldn't reach you on the phone, I borrowed a pistol from the desk of one of the intelligence officers and raced over." She started to hand over the weapon.

"Keep it. It might come in handy when you're leaving."

A stubborn expression crossed her face. "I'm staying with you. You might need help."

The woman was excess baggage at the moment, but it would be harder to convince her to leave than to let her stay.

He turned away from her and returned to the rear end of the roof. She followed him, whispering a question. "How are we going to get out of this?"

"Just watch," he said. "And keep quiet."

Lifting the M-16, he fitted a 40 mm fragmentation grenade on the M-203 launcher, then rested the weapon on the ledge of the roof wall and carefully sighted at the spot between the van and the men standing next to it.

He launched the missile, then grabbed Sirindikha's hand and pulled her down.

"Cover your head with your hands," he ordered.

A reverberating explosion echoed across the rear parking lot, followed by several eruptions as the fuel tank blew and ammo detonated.

The acrid stench of burning gasoline and charred flesh rose and filled the air.

The young embassy clerk looked as if she was going to vomit, then shoved a fist into her mouth and swallowed the bile.

She stared at Bolan in horror. "Did you have to kill them that way?"

"It was either that or die," Bolan replied.

He got to his feet and studied the scene through his binoculars. Except for some dents and scars from flying metal debris, his own car seemed to be intact. Nothing else was.

Bits of metal and body parts were scattered across the yard.

The passengers in the Mercedes-Benz were standing on the sidewalk. The lone survivor of the carnage raced out of an alley and headed for the well-dressed older man, spitting out a torrent of words.

Bolan saw the older man signal men from the truck. Four jumped from the rear and moved to his side. He pointed to the roof and issued orders.

Two raced back to the truck and returned with an RPG-2 rocket launcher, fitted with a Type 50 HEAT rocket.

"Time to get out of here," Bolan announced.

Leaving through the building was tantamount to committing suicide.

Peering over the roof ledge, he saw a rusty metal ladder attached to the side of the building. He lifted the canvas bag and leaned over the ledge. There was a small patch of grass near the bottom of the ladder. Bolan released the bag and watched it bounce on the soft area, then he surveyed the ground. Nobody had come back to the rear of the building. Not yet.

Shouldering the M-16, the big American gripped the Uzi in his right hand and climbed over the ledge and onto the top step.

"Follow me," he said to his companion, then began to work his way slowly down the steps.

Constantly peering into the darkness below, he searched for signs of the enemy coming for him. No one had yet.

He looked up and saw the embassy clerk descending above him. The heeled shoes she'd worn were not on her feet. Bolan gave her credit for common sense. He didn't need a woman with a broken neck right now.

Floor by floor he made his way to the ground, peering into every window he passed to make sure a sniper wasn't hiding inside.

Finally he reached the last metal step, which preceded a six-foot drop to the ground. Swinging by his left hand, he looked around to make sure nobody was waiting, then let go and let his feet hit the ground.

Jumping up, he made a half circle, Uzi in front of him, to survey the area.

Still empty.

Sirindikha was still five steps up when he heard the familiar whistling sound.

"Jump!" he shouted.

Without hesitation the young woman released her hold and fell. Bolan caught her around the waist, then pulled her against the building.

The roof of the building disintegrated as the rocket tore through it. Bricks and sandstone spun from the upper part of the apartment building at tornado speed.

"THEY ARE DEAD," Chen announced to his secretary.

"Yes, no one could survive such an explosion," she agreed.

"Now we can resume our search for the missing American diplomat," he commented. "When he is dead, we can go on with our—"

His comments were interrupted by the sound of squealing tires as a red Nissan sped out of the alley and swerved to avoid hitting the truck at the curb.

In fury the Chinese shouted orders. "Destroy that

car!'' Then he got into the Mercedes and waited impatiently for May Ling to jump in before roaring off in pursuit.

SIRINDIKHA SWERVED around the large truck and jammed her foot on the accelerator. She was driving so Bolan would be free to target any pursuers.

"We'd better burn rubber," Bolan urged.

Through the rear window he could see the truck straining to close the gap between them. Two men sat in the cab: the driver and a wide-faced Mongol. A third man had climbed up from the rear of the vehicle onto the roof. Carrying a large weapon, he pulled himself forward until he was on the top of the cab.

Bolan saw him steady his body and lift the weapon to his shoulder. The Executioner couldn't make out the piece, but he suspected it was one of the Chinese-manufactured 7.62 mm light submachine guns.

Bolan worked his way to the back and smashed the rear windshield out with the butt of his M-16.

The Mongolian in the passenger seat of the truck shoved an automatic rifle out the window.

While the young woman guided the car in a high-speed broken-field pattern to avoid the barrage of slugs from the two shooters, Bolan kept pumping lead from his assault rifle at the pursuing vehicle. Despite the hits he scored on the truck's front end with every round, he knew that even the powerful 5.56 mm rounds that he was firing would have difficulty destroying the radiator or engine of the large vehicle. And given their erratic path, it would be next to impossible for him to hit the tires of the truck.

Suddenly the searing light of a 40 mm incendiary grenade pitched from the truck exploded on the road between Bolan's vehicle and the pursuers, momentarily blinding him. Only the woman's sudden swerving prevented them from being overturned by the blast.

The Executioner had only a handful of rounds left in the M-16. There was no time to change magazines.

He carefully aimed at the top of the truck and showered it with a burst of 5.56 mm lead. The rooftop fighter suddenly released his hold on the submachine gun and grabbed for his face, rolling off into the road as he did.

Bolan pulled the M-16 back inside and, with one hand, changed magazines. Again he leaned the powerful assault weapon out of the window and aimed back at the passenger-side mirror of the pursuing truck. He heard the shriek of the shooter as lead ricocheted into the truck cab and burned into him.

Unmoved by the death of the man next to him, the truck driver kept pushing his vehicle closer.

Bolan unclipped a delay fragmentation grenade from his combat vest. Pulling the pin on the bomb, he carefully rolled it back at the oncoming vehicle.

The ear-shattering explosion sent waves of steel fragments tearing through the floor of the front end of the truck, then the vehicle swerved off the road and ran into a ditch.

"Stop the car," Bolan ordered, "and get down behind it."

Grabbing the fully loaded Uzi submachine gun, he shoved open the rear door and jumped outside as three bleeding assailants ran toward him, firing their weapons.

The soldier had no time to stop to take careful aim. He washed the kill zone in front of him with waves of 9 mm death, then watched as the trio crumpled to the ground, twitching before they lay still.

Bolan dived for cover as he heard the sound of an automatic weapon being fired in his direction.

One survivor had taken cover behind the destroyed truck.

Elbowing his way forward, the Executioner worked his way around to the right side of the stopped truck.

Pausing to snap a fresh magazine into the Uzi, he continued his crawling until he had a clear vision of the assailant.

It was the older, well-dressed man who seemed to be in charge, and he'd crept up from where the Mercedes was parked. In his hands was an American-made .45-caliber Ingram Model 10 SMG, rather than one of the Chinese weapons.

"Drop the gun, Chen," Bolan shouted.

The Chinese intelligence agent's response was a wave of heavy lead poured in the direction of the soldier's voice, but by then Bolan had moved five feet to the right.

He had given the Chinese colonel a chance to surrender. Time was up.

The big American stood and pumped lead into his fury-faced adversary. Lead shredded the agent's impeccably tailored suit and chiseled holes in his chest and stomach. Blood spurted through the large tears in his clothing, drenching him.

There was a clicking sound behind him; a hammer was being pulled back.

Slowly he turned. A handsome Chinese woman stood behind him, holding an American-made .357 Magnum Colt Python revolver.

"You die, American bastard!" she yelled.

A pair of shots exploded, and the expression on the Chinese woman's face changed from hate to surprise. Then she lost all expression as she fell forward to the ground.

Chandra Sirindikha was holding the H&K pistol with both hands, staring in shock at the dead body on the ground near her.

Without a word the pale-faced woman handed the weapon to Bolan.

"I don't like this part of the job," she whispered. "I never thought that I would ever have to kill."

"When the choice is between you and them, there's only one possible decision," he said in sympathy.

19

The word filtered back to the Tamil chieftain about his sister's death.

"How did she die?"

His aide hesitated, then replied. "Sirimavo died well. She swallowed a cyanide capsule."

"Lalith, why did she take the capsule?"

"Does it matter, Thamby?"

"Yes, it does."

"She had been tortured by camp guards."

"Then how did she find the free moment for the capsule?"

"According to what was reported to us from contacts in the prison camp, some American broke in and killed the torturers."

The Tamil Tiger head knew who the man was. Michael Belasko. He had instructed Madi Kirbal to give him the information about his sister.

The American had failed to save the Indian woman or his sister. The penalty for failure was death.

"Lalith, do we know how to find this American?"

"No, but we know he has been friendly with a clerk at the American Embassy. We can bring her in," Lalith offered.

Thamby weighed the suggestion. "No, that might enrage the Americans even more. Have her followed."

He thought of something else. "How did the Boosa butchers know which one of their prisoners was my sister?"

"Someone must have told them," his aide commented. "Perhaps someone who has a member of their family being held in the camp."

Thamby nodded. "I want a complete list of every Tiger who has family interned in the Boosa camp."

As Bolan waited for the young embassy woman to come out of her apartment building on the south end of the city, he felt the presence of danger. Looking around in the intense late-afternoon sunlight, he saw no one watching him. Only a moving van, parked at the curb.

Sirindikha walked out of the front door, dressed in a short black cocktail dress, and hurried down the steps, running until she reached Bolan's car.

Getting in, she looked at him. "You look very presentable in civilian clothes," she commented admiringly.

She had suggested Bolan buy some clothes at a department store suitable to attend a high-level birthday party. He had insisted that the fitter make one concession, despite the tailor's loud objection.

The jacket had to be loose-fitting. He didn't explain to the small Englishman that the garment had to accommodate a shoulder holster.

As he started the engine, he said, "Before we parted company last night, you mentioned a contact you had in Jaffna. Were you able to reach him?"

"He was out of the city on business. I'll try him again later."

Pulling away from the curb, he asked her to guide him to Bandaran's estate.

"It's on the north end, about twenty miles outside of the city." She suggested they get on the highway edging Colombo. "There's hardly ever any traffic on it after the local rush hour."

Glancing in the rearview mirror, Bolan saw the moving van pull away from the curb. As they drove slowly through the city traffic, he kept looking in the side-view mirror.

The van was still behind them. The Executioner wondered if it was a coincidence or was it following them.

The wariness returned. Bolan didn't believe in co-incidences.

As they approached the highway, he decided to slow and see if it passed him. It maintained its position behind him.

Glancing back, he saw the two expressionless men wearing fatigues in the front seats.

Trying not to alarm his companion, he eased the Beretta from under his jacket and tucked it between his thighs.

Traffic was almost nonexistent. Only one car—a small Toyota sedan—was coming toward him on the opposite side of the road. There were no vehicles behind the truck.

Bolan pushed down hard on the gas pedal, and the compact embassy car raced forward.

Sirindikha was shoved back by the sudden acceleration, and she started to ask a question, then stopped when she saw the grim expression on his face. Instead she turned her head and looked out the rear window.

He heard the roar of a powerful engine, and looking

in the side-view mirror, Bolan saw that the large vehicle was moving quickly to catch up.

Now he knew. The young woman and he were the targets. Or, at least, one of them was.

He could slam on the brakes, jump out and try to eliminate the two men following him. But there was always the chance that a stray slug would hit his companion.

The risk was too great. He'd have to outrun them.

He could hear the protesting squeal of tires behind him as the other driver tried to keep up with his erratic bursts of speed.

The woman turned quickly from the rear window and looked at Bolan. "What's that they're holding out the window?"

He glanced in his rearview mirror. A flash of reflected sunlight bounced off a metal object being held out of the front window of the van. Bolan couldn't make out what kind of gun it was. Probably a 9 mm Uzi or Skorpion.

He didn't waste time worrying about the brand. It didn't matter. Either could kill.

Over the rush of wind slamming against his car, he could hear the soft thud of slugs glancing off his vehicle.

Trying as hard as he could, the Executioner couldn't pull away from the van. He had decided to try another tactic. He jammed on the brakes.

The pursuit vehicle almost slammed into his back end, then swerved and moved up to parallel his window.

Steering one-handed, Bolan shoved the Beretta out his window. As he emptied the clip at the other vehicle, he saw the wide-faced man framed in the opened passenger window drop his submachine gun and grab for his cheek and scream at the sudden pain.

The soldier couldn't risk an accident by taking his eyes off the road. Guessing at the direction, he rapidly pumped two more rounds at the sound of the screaming man.

He heard the plinking sound of brass cases bouncing against his door, and the high-pitched whine as one of the slugs ricocheted from the edge of the window, deep into the man's left eye.

As he risked glancing at the van briefly, Bolan saw the man slide down out of view.

The driver, an angry-looking man with a scar traversing his face, raised his subgun and started to fire wildly at the Nissan. The big American tried to return fire, but heard the ominous click of metal hitting metal.

There was no time to drop the empty clip and snap in a new one. All he could do was try to outrun the other car.

"Lean back!" Sirindikha shouted.

He felt a burning tail of lead sear the air in front of his face as he pushed his head back against the rest on his seat. Two 9 mm parabellum slugs flew through the open window and hit the narrow metal trim around the other vehicle's window.

Bolan glanced at the young embassy clerk and saw the compact 9 mm automatic she was steadying in her hands. Her eyes were hard, shiny balls of light, focused on the car to his left.

All the Executioner could do to help was to keep the two vehicles parallel.

"Hang on," he yelled as he twisted the steering wheel from one side to the other, trying to close the gap between the two vehicles.

Out of the corner of his eye, he saw his companion fire three more rounds at their adversaries. The driver of the van slumped forward, as if he had just decided he needed to take a nap, and the driverless vehicle started to swerve out of control.

"Brace yourself," Bolan shouted as he slammed on the brakes and let the other vehicle pull ahead.

Like an enraged elephant, the van went berserk, twisting its way in a sinuous motion across the road, narrowly missing a donkey pulling a wagon coming in the opposite direction.

As the soldier and the woman watched, the metallic behemoth crashed at full speed into a wire barrier on the edge of the road, stopping momentarily. Suddenly the gas tank ruptured and exploded into a brilliant ball of flame.

A body flew through the metal framework that had once held a front windshield and rolled across the road, stopping a few feet from the embassy car.

Bolan rammed a fresh clip into the Beretta, shoved open his door and got out, Sirindikha mirroring him on the other side of the vehicle. Together they cautiously approached the still form on the ground.

The Executioner nudged the body with a toe. Satisfied the gunman wasn't playing dead, he kneeled and turned him over. What remained of the face was covered with blood-soaked dirt. Much of the neck had been shot away.

He looked at the overturned van and saw the other body trapped inside the twisted metal, then turned and glanced at the embassy clerk. Her face revealed no emotions, but he sensed she was satisfied.

Bolan understood how she had to feel. He had felt the same way many times. Killing was an ugly but necessary part of his job. He didn't have to like doing it, but when it had to be done, better that it was him doing it to someone else than having someone else do it to him.

It was the philosophy of professionals who sometimes had to kill in the line of duty. It was his philosophy. And he now had no doubts that Chandra Sirindikha was a professional.

They heard the roar of approaching engines. He tapped her arm and pointed to the battered Nissan.

They got in and drove away before anyone arrived and started asking questions. Neither one of them spoke as Bolan pointed the vehicle in the direction of the suburb where the minister of internal security lived. There wasn't anything to say. At least, not until they found out which one of them had been the target.

And why.

IN A BUILDING on the edge of the city of Jaffna, near the string of islets that led to the state of Tamil Nadu, a middle-aged man was being questioned.

"No, please. Not again!" Samil Tambimuttu watched in terror as the short, wide, bare-chested man moved toward him again. He still gripped the two copper rods in his rubber-gloved hands.

The thin man struggled with the chains that held him to the slimy brick wall. He could feel the torture of the metal chafing against his open wounds his wrists had become. Turning his head, he could see the two thick wires that attached the copper sticks to a truck battery sitting on the ground.

He screamed out the question for a hundredth time. "What did I do?"

There was no response to the plea. He tried to see

who was standing in the shadows across the room, but it was too dark.

His eyes opened wider as the copper weapons moved closer

"No!" he screeched as surges of electricity tore through his genitals.

The searing fire made his body jerk as it burned its way through his nervous system. He started to weep.

He could hear voices whisper from the shadows. He shouted out desperately, "Who are you? Why are you doing this to me?"

They had brought him to the stone building just outside of Jaffna in the afternoon and spent the next several hours asking him about his brother, who was a prisoner in the Boosa Camp.

"I have never heard from him since the government arrested him. I swear!"

It was obvious they didn't believe him. When night came, they led him down a narrow flight of stairs into a windowless basement. He could smell the stale stench of a room that had never been exposed to fresh air.

Despite the closeness of the room, he could feel the dampness from outside creeping through the concrete blocks that formed the outer walls.

He looked down at himself. The precious suit he had saved up for two years to buy was torn and covered with blood. His blood!

Where was he? He had never seen a place like this. It was like a dungeon in hell.

Who would do such a thing to a simple man like himself? Perhaps the Tiger leadership blamed him for leaking information about them. But he hadn't. He had nothing to share.

It had to be the Tigers. But what did they want?

He began to shiver with the fear of suddenly knowing where he was. This was an interrogation room of the Tigers. He had heard what happened to others brought to such places.

He stared at the man with the copper rods. He had to know if this had something to do with his hotheaded brother. He had begged him not to become a guerrilla. His brother had to have told someone what he had said.

"Are you the Tigers?"

"Yes."

The word came from a figure hidden in the shadows of the room.

"I am innocent. There must be some mistake. I am a loyal Tamil. I voted for the Tamil candidates in the last election," he cried.

"The Tigers never make mistakes," the voice replied.

The bare-chested man wiped the sweat from his forehead. His hairy chest was drenched with perspiration. He turned away and peered into the darkness, then turned back, as if he had been given additional instructions, and rammed the rods against the sides of his victim's neck.

It seemed as if a thousand snakes had bitten him. His body leaped into the air, trying to escape the waves of unimaginable agony.

He screeched, and the rods pulled away. He let his head slump. Maybe he wouldn't have to wake again.

The sweating man studied his face. "He is unconscious, Commander," he called out.

A figure emerged from the shadows. It was a small man, in his fifties, dressed in tailored fatigues. Jayewar

Vamil stared at the chained form, then turned to the man holding the electrical rods.

Vamil was one of Thamby's key aides. He helped the Tamil leader run the guerrilla camps around the city of Jaffna. "Tell me when you think he's ready to be questioned," he told the interrogator.

"He'll be unconscious for at least five minutes."

"That long?" A second figure emerged from the shadows. He was a tall, thin man with hardened features. Like the smaller man, he was wearing fatigues, only his looked as though he'd slept in them.

"At least that long," the interrogator replied with certainty. He had been an interrogator for the Tigers for more than fifteen years. Visitors didn't often come to view his work. Not one as prominent as the heavy-set man.

He had recognized him immediately. He was one of the three supreme commanders of the Tigers, Rajiv Thamby.

"We'll wait," Thamby said, sighing.

"I don't think he knows anything," Vamil commented.

The stout man leaned over and spoke softly. "We must be absolutely certain that he did not pass on information to the STP in exchange for certain privileges his brother has received from them."

"Get him ready for questioning," Vamil ordered.

Nodding, the other man picked up the copper sticks and touched them to each other. Sparks exploded as they made contact.

He stepped close to the chained man. "Open your eyes, traitorous scum," he snarled, and rammed the charged rods against his eyeballs.

The chained man screamed.

"My eyes! My eyes! I'm blind!"

Vamil walked to him. "Do you remember someone coming to you and telling you your brother could get better treatment if you provided them with information about the Tigers?"

The man whimpered in reply. "Somebody contacted me from the police. But I wouldn't tell them anything."

The uniformed man leaned close to his face. "Your brother lives apart from the other prisoners in the Boosa camp. He receives better food and better treatment. Why?"

"I don't know," the banker wept.

"Next we'll do your ears. Talk!"

The threat spurred the prisoner's voice to become audible. "I told the man who contacted me that I knew nothing about the Tigers that was useful."

"Then what happened?"

"He gave me a telephone number in Colombo and told me to call it whenever I heard anything about the guerrillas, no matter how insignificant."

"Did you?"

"Only once," the tortured man pleaded.

"What did you tell him?"

"Something I heard from a customer in the bank. It wasn't important. About an American who was coming to talk to the Tigers about a truce." He broke down and started to cry. "But I told the man that it was only a rumor."

"Did you tell your wife about the rumor? Or your young son?"

"No!" The man started to weep again. "They know nothing."

Vamil's tone was suddenly gentle. "Not even a casual mention?"

"No. nothing. I swear it!"

The area commander was satisfied. He turned to the interrogator.

"I'm finished with him."

He strode from the room into the dark, wet corridor. The tall, thin man followed him out.

Thamby talked as if he were thinking out loud. "Even among the Tigers there are those who would betray us." He pointed to the door of the interrogation room. "Like the banker in there."

"But even if this American negotiator exists, no one knows where he is," Vamil said.

"I do. He is in my camp, just west of the city."

For the Tiger chieftain, the nightmare had started after his men had taken the American prisoner. STF agents offered a variety of incentives, ranging from money to freeing relatives in their slave camps, for information on where the Tigers had taken the man.

Thamby knew that what worried the Sinhalese government in Colombo was that the Tigers might be talking about a real truce.

A truce could cost the minister of internal security an important portion of his income. The money the fat official received from contraband smugglers for closing his eyes to their efforts was deposited in a bank account outside of the country, from what the Tiger leader's spies had reported.

Allan Bandaran had spies, as well, men he paid to pass on vital information about the plans and movements of the rebel armies, information that had cost the lives of many loyal soldiers.

Not that the Tigers were ready for peace. They had

fought the Sinhalese too long to just stop. More blood had to be shed to atone for the sins the Buddhists had committed on the Tamils before he would agree to that.

From inside, Thamby could hear the screams of the chained man, drowning out the exploding sparks of electricity. After a few minutes there was only silence.

The interrogator came out of the room, pulling on a thick work shirt as he walked to the two waiting men.

"Done." He looked at the Jaffna commander for further orders. "Anything else you want, sir?"

Thamby knew the identities of most of those who had sold out the cause to the government.

Vamil smiled at the Tiger chieftain. "Anything else you need from my man or me?"

He waited for an answer, but Thamby said nothing.

The aide turned to walk away. He had a call to make. His mother would continue to receive preferred treatment at the Boosa Camp when he notified the STF that Thamby had the missing diplomat in his Jaffna camp.

"Just one more thing," the Tiger chief said quietly.

Vamil turned back. "Yes?"

"I want the truth," Thamby said quietly.

The aide looked puzzled. "About what?"

"Why you agreed to work for Bandaran's killers."

A look of shock covered the local Tiger boss's face. He began to deny the accusation, then looked down at Thamby's right hand, which held a 9 mm SIG-Sauer pistol.

Thamby slowly squeezed the trigger twice while Vamil tried to protest his innocence.

"It isn't true—"

Two soft-nosed slugs chewed a path into the STF's informant. Without finishing the sentence, he slid to the floor. Only his eyes showed his confusion.

"Traitors have to die," Thamby explained calmly. "When they find your body, your death will be blamed on the special task force, which makes sense because your men have killed so many of them."

The Tiger chief kneeled and pushed the pistol into the fallen man's ear, then squeezed the trigger and jumped back as gray-white brain pulp spurted from the jagged opening.

Slipping his automatic back into his pocket, Thamby stood and turned to the interrogator. There was a stunned expression on the man's face, which vanished when he realized his commander was staring at him.

"Call somebody to get rid of the bodies."

Thamby started to leave, then stopped and added another demand.

"Have some men sent to bring in the wife and child for questioning. And see if the prisoner told them anything."

He looked at his watch. It was time to call the two men who shared the command of the rebel movement about the dead traitor.

The two men, Neelan and Konamalai, had antiquated ideas about running a rebellion. They still believed that the soldiers should be treated with love and respect. But Thamby knew that the only thing that the Tamil Tigers would respect was the torture they would be subjected to if they didn't obey commands. Thamby knew that some day the three of them would have to resolve their differences. Even if it meant his having to kill the other two.

To tell them the truth about Vamil would require too long an explanation. He had a simpler story planned.

STF forces had invaded Jaffna, found Commander Vamil and tried to torture him for information. But the commander, always faithful to the Tiger cause, refused to tell them anything. So the STF mercenaries killed him.

Thamby would promise the others that he would pursue the assassins until they were caught and killed. Even at the risk of his own safety.

20

The fishing-boat captain sat in the saloon on the Madras waterfront, sipping a lager beer and feeling sorry for himself. He had information worth thousands of rupees, and no one to whom to sell it.

Chen was dead. So was Atwater.

All he was going to get was the money the Americans were paying him to pick up the large foreigner on Whelped Beach the following night.

There had to be somebody who wanted to know about the rendezvous. Perhaps those Sinhalese maniacs who worked for the special task force. Or perhaps the Tamils.

Maybe both of them would like to know, for a price. Suddenly he started feeling better.

He had contacts in both groups. Of course, he would insist on payment up front. There was no sense in trusting people with something as fragile as information.

He dug some bills from his pocket and went to the bar to get change for the telephone.

CHANDRA SIRINDIKHA pulled her small car to a stop at the gateway of the large house. An STF officer approached her and looked inside.

"Invitation, please," he said, holding out his hand.

She handed over the engraved card Bolan had found in Madi Kirbal's apartment.

"Your name?"

"Chandra Sirindikha, of the United States Embassy."

The STF hardman looked past her at the man in the passenger seat. "And you are?"

"This is Mr. Daniel Boone," she replied, smiling.

The uniformed guard studied the large man sitting next to the young woman. Satisfied, he pointed to a roped-off area.

"Park there," he ordered.

As they got out of the car, Bolan looked at her. "Daniel Boone?"

"I had to think of a name fast," she said. "And don't complain. We're in."

"You still haven't explained where you learned to shoot like that," Bolan commented.

"I don't suppose you'd believe Fresno Community College," she said, trying to soften the tension between them.

"Not this time."

"This isn't the right moment to discuss it," she replied. "For now let's concentrate on why we're here."

A range of possibilities that started with the CIA and traversed the intelligence services of foreign countries popped into Bolan's mind. Remembering Kirbal, Bolan reminded himself that she could be working for more than one side. But the young woman was right. This wasn't the time or place to think about it.

The Executioner forced himself to focus on the reasons they were here.

"I don't suppose any of the Tamil big shots are going to be here," he said.

"I wouldn't think so," she replied, looking at the armed STF troops around the huge living room. "But you never know."

ALLAN BANDARAN was furious. If the president hadn't decided to show up at the last minute, his birthday party would have been a smashing success. Especially if his guest showed up, as promised.

However, he couldn't tell the head of the government to go home.

Simon Alphamundai was a weak-spined coward. Bandaran had tried to get him to declare war on the Tamils, but the old man refused to do so. He kept confusing achieving peace with selling out his own people. Bandaran knew that real peace could only be achieved when the Tamils were all dead or driven from Sri Lanka.

He was building support among the politicians in office for that inevitable day. Alphamundai wouldn't live forever, and there was no one more qualified than the minister of internal security to step up to the presidency.

All it would take were a few more raids by the Tamils on Sinhalese civilians, and the outcry for Alphamundai to step down would echo through the country.

Bandaran knew he was close to having enough backing to assume the post.

He greeted the president and had one of the STF officers lead him to the refreshment table. In such a large group he supposed he could ignore Alphamundai's presence.

Across the room a petite, attractive woman was talking to a tall, ragged-looking European or American.

The man looked familiar. Bandaran knew he had seen him before, but couldn't remember where.

A large group of men and women walked into the foyer. The minister promptly forgot about the man and painted a smile on his face, preparing to greet his guests.

SIRINDIKHA'S EYES followed the minister as he walked toward the front door.

"There he goes, Sri Lanka's walking bank account. Nothing illegal happens in this country if he doesn't get a percentage."

"Like the Mafia."

"Just like them. Only he's all the Mafia gangs rolled into one."

Bolan looked at the short, slim man with whom Bandaran had been talking.

"One of the minister's cronies?"

"Hardly. Simon Alphamundai is the country's president and supposed to be a decent guy for a politician. I think Bandaran was forced on him by his political party."

"At least it seems they agree on eliminating the Tamils," the soldier commented.

"They don't agree on anything. Not even that. The president has publicly said that he thinks the Tamils should have a part of the country they can control. His only condition is that it be an integral part of Sri Lanka."

Bolan's attention was drawn by Bandaran's movements.

The minister walked over to one of the STF officers,

whispered something in the uniformed man's ear, then walked into a private room.

Bolan wondered why the security minister had left the party.

"Something going on in there?"

"It wouldn't surprise me. Almost everyone in the government takes payoffs," she whispered, "especially Allan Bandaran and his STF cronies."

IT HAD BEEN a very profitable year, Bandaran reflected as he waited for his visitor to slip into the room. The ground-floor window had been left open for easy access, and the STF guards had been ordered to stay away from the area around it.

Even with the intrusion by the Americans trying to force peace on the country, his numbered account in Zurich continued to grow.

Yes, a very successful year. And soon to be even more successful, he reminded himself as he watched the tall, dark-skinned man climb through the window.

Rajiv Thamby was one of the reasons he had decided to throw himself a birthday party. Through intermediaries, the Tamil rebel leader had contacted him about buying guns and ammunition.

For Bandaran, getting the arms to sell to the Tiger leader was simple. The government warehouses had more than enough supplies, and he controlled the warehouses.

THE TAMIL LEADER SMILED. He wanted to kill the little fat man facing him, for the sake of his sister. But the cause came first, even before revenge for her. There would be time to make the filthy animal pay for his crimes.

But for now the Tigers needed replenishments of weapons and ammunition. Thamby had dealt with men like Bandaran. The Chinese colonel had wanted assurances that the Liberation Tigers supported his country's Communist philosophy. In exchange for supplies, the Indians had demanded he promise loyalty to their government. The only good thing he'd gotten from New Delhi was Madi Kirbal and her willingness to serve the cause.

The Tamil leader was willing to promise anything to get the desperately needed arms.

"You'll have the supplies as soon as we receive the money," the stout man promised. Then he added, "But we won't deliver them. We'll leave them for your men to pick up at some remote location."

"How much do you want for the supplies?"

Bandaran quoted a price and saw the stunned expression on the Tamil's face.

"That is ten times what they are worth," Thamby snarled.

"Where else can you get arms and ammunition this fast?"

Thamby knew the Sinhalese minister was right. There were only a handful of arms dealers willing to do business with the Tamil terrorist army. And the most important one, Henry Chen, was dead. So was Clay Atwater, who'd been reliable, if greedy.

But there was something about the man before him that filled Thamby with anger. It wasn't just the exorbitant amount he was demanding, nor the slaughter of a young, innocent woman or Madi Kirbal. There was something unclean about him, as if he were covered with the sores of a leper.

"No," the Tamil leader decided. "If you decide to ask a more reasonable price, I will come back."

The minister smiled. "And if you change your mind, have someone contact me," he replied.

But Bandaran knew the Tiger chief would never be able to do that. Preparing for the probability of not being able to make a deal, Bandaran had stationed a large squad of his best STF soldiers in the wooded area backing onto the rear of his house.

They would wait until the Tamil crossed the lawn before commencing the attack, and *he* would be leading them. Bandaran could see the headlines: Minister Of Internal Security Leads Assault That Kills Tamil Terrorist Leader.

BOLAN WAITED for the young woman to unlock the car doors, then slid into the passenger seat. He could feel the eyes of the STF guard, acting as parking director, drilling through his clothes.

Allan Bandaran came out of the front door and led a well-dressed English couple to a Bentley. He watched as the two drove away, then turned and started to walk toward the side of his large house.

Stopping, he turned back and stared at Bolan through the windshield of Sirindikha's car. The soldier eased his hand under his jacket and let it rest near the shoulder rig.

The minister shook his head and turned away, then walked briskly around the building until he vanished from sight.

Sirindikha had been holding her breath. Now she could exhale. "That was close," she said, shivering over the memory of the minister's piercing stare. The young woman took her hands from the wheel and looked at the warrior. "Before we leave, I want you to know that I'm going north with you."

"It's too dangerous."

"You need me," she replied. "I saved your neck on the street outside of your apartment building."

The Executioner had to admit that she had reacted quickly.

"Don't you have to show up for work?"

"I can take a sick day."

"Call me tomorrow," he said, knowing he'd be driving north to meet the fishing boat captain before she was awake.

The young woman backed out of the parking space, then spun the steering wheel and drove onto the roadway.

A tall, dark-faced man dressed in fatigues came out of the shadows. He stopped and stared into the embassy car, then continued his journey across the road to a waiting van.

Bolan saw the puzzled expression on his companion's face.

"Something wrong?"

"The man who came from behind Bandaran's house was Rajiv Thamby, the leader of the Tigers, or his double," she said, still looking confused.

The chattering of a dozen automatic weapons startled them. For a moment Bolan thought he was the target. Then he saw uniformed STF troops charge across the lawn toward the van. Bolan recognized them as mercenaries, and at their head was Allan Bandaran.

The Executioner unleathered the silenced Beretta 93-R and exited the car, followed by Sirindikha.

"Let's take cover," he stated, leading the way to a stand of trees between the house and the roadway.

As they crouched and watched, a dozen rebels appeared magically from behind trees and bushes.

Returning the STF gunfire with bursts of lead from a battery of AK-47s, the guerrilla fighters had the advantage of not having to shoot while in motion.

With deadly accuracy they found their targets. Eight of the STF soldiers fell, shredded by the unending storm of lead.

A whistle blew, and six more STF-uniformed troops rushed across the roadway to aid their comrades. Brandishing submachine guns, they emptied their weapons at the group of fighters bordering the stopped van.

Four of the Tamils fell to the ground, bleeding. Another spun as a hail of lead chiseled into his body, pushing him back into a tree, where he died.

Undaunted by the surprise assault, the Tamil fighters stood their ground, emptying their weapons at the ever-diminishing number of attackers.

One by one the government soldiers surrendered their lives to the barrage of 7.62 mm rounds.

"Turn slowly."

The voice behind Bolan surprised him. He turned and saw the stout government official pointing a SIG-Sauer pistol at him and his companion.

Bandaran grabbed the young woman by the arm and yanked her away.

"You come with me," he said, his voice filled with panic.

"I'm with the United States government," she protested.

"Right now you're my shield." He backed away from Bolan, keeping his hostage between them.

"Drop your gun," Bandaran ordered, glaring at the big American.

The Executioner let the Beretta fall to his side, then moved backward and seemed to trip. As he fell, the minister moved his hand to aim the weapon in the soldier's direction.

Bolan rolled to his right as Bandaran fired twice.

With a swift movement the Executioner spit a continuous spray of lead at his adversary. The rounds tore Bandaran into shreds of splintered bone and tissue. Blood spurted from ten cavities, tinting the green lawn with a layer of red.

Across the road the Tamil leader stared at Bolan for a brief moment, then got into the van and drove out of there.

Bolan shoved the Beretta back into its holster. Glancing at the tattered corpse near him, he felt only relief that another cannibal had been laid to rest.

As he helped Sirindikha to her feet and led her back to the car, he had only one regret. He had wanted to corner the Tamil chief and force him to reveal where John Vu was being held. But there'd be another time for that confrontation.

Perhaps as soon as tomorrow.

21

The drive north had been long and dull. As he passed the still-dark huts that lined Highway 3, he thought about the embassy clerk. She was a strange mixture of naiveté and shrewdness. Without any apparent training, she seemed to know how to handle herself in tense situations.

Abruptly switching focus, he considered his course of action. He would drop his carryall near the beach, then drive to the tourist facilities in Whelped and leave his car there. He had called the administration office for the national park from Colombo and asked if someone could drive him to the beach.

The reaction was one of surprise.

"This is the rainy season, the wrong time to come here," the woman on the other end had replied. "In a few days the beach will be six inches under water, and you'll drown."

"I know. But my editor wants me to photograph how the monsoon affects wildlife in Whelped," Bolan told her.

Reluctantly she agreed to store his car and drive him to the shore.

WAITING IN THE JUNGLE that bordered the beach, Bolan watched as the clouds gathered and became a solid thickness in the sky. In a few days all of this area would become a marshlands, unnavigable.

He opened his bag, took out the Beretta 93-R and slid it into the shoulder holster hidden under the oversize rain slicker he'd just bought in Colombo. The .44-caliber Desert Eagle slipped easily into the rigid leather holster on his belt. The Applegate-Fairbairn combat knife sat in the sheath strapped to his left arm.

The combat vest under the knee-high raincoat held various weapons of war: full clips for the two handguns, for the M–16 and M-203 combo, and the silenced Uzi submachine gun. M-40 delay fragmentation and incendiary grenades were attached to metal clips. He had chosen the M-16 as his main piece.

The big American carefully peered into the jungle that surrounded him and listened for sounds of an enemy.

The dense growth was alive with noises of living creatures. He could hear the sounds of the birds, and small animals scurrying along the ground, searching for food.

A profusion of trees, shrubs, wildflowers and exotic plants competed with one another for space in the thickly populated wilderness. Bright, almost-electrified blotches of color from the different tropical plants vied for Bolan's attention.

He knew—not guessed—knew that somebody was waiting for the right moment to strike.

A slight sound became audible, coming from behind the nearby trees. Bolan turned to see where the sound originated and saw a half-dozen black-clad men running toward him, screaming guttural curses in Tamil as they did. He could see the blood lust in their expressions as they recklessly charged through the jungle from a hundred yards away, their AK-47s spraying a wall of lead in his direction.

These weren't trained fighters, or they would have held their fire until they were close enough for the rounds to hit their target.

Him.

Bolan raced into the forest behind him. It was a poor shield. The trees offered little protection against high-powered ammunition, but at least they provided him with temporary cover until he could calculate his next move.

The soldier tried to decide who had sent them. Sirindikha? Not unless he'd totally misjudged her. Perhaps the woman at the Whelped tourist facility?

The answer was suddenly obvious.

The fishing-boat captain. He was a mercenary, and mercenaries sold information to anyone willing to pay them.

Bolan decided he would deal with the man after he was delivered to Jaffna, but before the informer could notify his other customers where the soldier was heading.

The Executioner was grateful that he said he'd give the captain his destination after they got under way.

Meanwhile he'd have to make his stand here.

Like a wraith Bolan streaked toward the startled guerrillas, throwing an M-40 frag grenade, then switching to a two-handed grip on the M-16. As the bomb ripped the center flank of the enemy, shrill cries of agony shattered the stillness of the night. The handful of shadows started to vanish behind trees.

Someone hollered something in a strange tongue, which Bolan assumed was Tamil. The guerrillas stopped and turned back.

Six remained alive. Clad in a mixture of peasant and combat attire, they wore crude straw hats and elephant-ear leaves across their shoulders to protect them from the rain.

Obedience rather than combat skill seemed to spark their willingness to risk their lives for the Tigers.

The first of the group charged in a burst of bravado, accompanied by loud shouting, and he raised his assault rifle.

Bolan set his M-16 on burst mode, tracked the movement of the lead attacker and fired. The volley of bullets drilled into the guerrilla and punched him to the jungle floor. The Executioner turned to face another charging gunner.

Firing on the move, the hardman emptied the clip of his assault rifle. Bolan rolled away, firing as he did.

His first shot carved a path through his enemy's side, while the second severed the large artery in his neck. The would-be assassin fell to the ground, the rain diluting his life fluid and forming a thin red pool around the body.

The four surviving terrorists fled back into the forest, but not for long. He could hear the shouts of the remaining guerrillas as they challenged one another to lead another attack on the American.

Finally the quartet moved closer together, then forward, spraying a path of 7.62 mm death as they advanced.

Bolan hurried to the right and hunched down to wait until the four came closer, then jumped to his feet, gripping the M-16 combo in both hands. He didn't waste time sighting the rifle, setting the weapon on automatic and firing the powerhouse rounds from the hip. The four black-clad fighters stayed vertical for a moment, held in place by the impact of several rounds. Then they dropped lifeless to the ground.

Carefully approaching then kicking the weapons away from the bodies, Bolan crouched and felt the neck artery of each before being satisfied that they were truly dead. This guerrilla hit squad would never ambush anyone again.

Behind him in the bush, the Executioner heard the sounds of a coughing engine. Stealthily moving through the undergrowth, he saw a surplus military jeep and two fatigue-clad soldiers. They were studying the bodies of the first two terrorists he'd killed.

The tall man in the passenger seat reached for a radio mike mounted on the dashboard, and Bolan suspected he was going to call for backup.

In an easy motion the Executioner raised the M-16 combo to his shoulder and carefully looked through the sight.

Fifty yards separated him from the vehicle. In a matter of minutes, help would be on the way.

Releasing the frag grenade, Bolan dropped to the ground, let the combo fall from his hands and covered his head with his hands.

He could hear the ear-shattering explosion as grenade met jeep and consumed it in a hurricane-force hail of shredded metal. Waiting to let the fragments settle to the ground, Bolan finally got to his feet and looked toward where the surplus vehicle had been standing.

Only the car frame was intact. The other parts had scattered in different directions. Bolan doubted the terrorist had had time to contact his command center before he was chewed up by the hurtling metal shards.

The Executioner picked up his canvas carryall and walked toward the beach.

He waved a hand above his head and waited for a raft to come to get him.

22

Only the sound of an occasional fish rising to the surface to jump at some resting bug broke the silence. Bolan leaned on the ship's rail and stared at the water, dark and running swiftly, pushed by a breeze.

Under the fatigues he was wearing his one-piece blacksuit and his weapons. He hardly felt the weight and bulk of the Beretta 93-R, the massive Desert Eagle or the Applegate-Fairbairn combat knife.

As it had before, the vessel reeked of dead fish and garbage. There was no pretense of keeping the craft clean. Heavy ropes that usually tethered fishing nets hung loosely from heavy metal rings mounted beneath the railing.

Bolan glanced briefly at them, then returned to more pressing thoughts. The mission was far from being finished. But at least now he had some idea where to find the American diplomat.

Chandra Sirindikha had finally talked to her contact up north, who'd heard that Vu was being held in a small village just outside of Jaffna. Bolan would be met at the dock by the contact, who would be able to supply him with further details.

"My contact said he was willing to get involved. He'll be waiting on the dock, and he'll know your name."

Bolan felt a pair of eyes drilling into his back. Turning, he caught the fishing-boat captain staring at him.

"Something wrong?"

"No, no," the captain replied hastily. "I was just wondering how long you planned to stay in Jaffna."

"I believe that's my business," Bolan stated bluntly.

"Of course, of course," the captain said, and hurried away.

The big American studied the first mate and the other two members of the crew. All three looked more like hit men than sailors.

The crew sensed his attention and moved out of sight.

Through the thinning mist, Bolan saw the vague shadows of buildings. Jaffna. They'd be there shortly.

THE CAPTAIN STOOD near the door to his cabin, smiling as he heard one of the crew whisper a complaint to the man standing next to him.

"All we do is sail back and forth from Tamil Nadu to Sri Lanka. I signed on to fish, not transport illegals. If the border guards catch us, we could spend years in some stinking prison."

The captain decided it was time to share some of the fifty thousand rupees he'd been promised by his Tamil contact for killing the American. Perhaps he'd give each of them a thousand rupees, more than either earned in a month. And that would leave him with forty-eight thousand to add to his small but growing bank account.

He turned his head and signaled his mate, a stocky man with a huge black mustache.

"Keep an eye on those two," he said quietly. "I'm not sure we can trust either of them."

The taciturn mate nodded and returned to coiling a length of rope on the deck.

The captain had a signal to send. He had promised the man who had hired him to notify him when the target was aboard.

Glancing at the American, he wondered if the man knew how little time he had left. Since he'd first transported the man a few days earlier, he wondered what was in the canvas bag sitting at the man's feet.

Perhaps money. Or expensive weapons. Or both.

It didn't matter. The contents would be his when the American was dead and floating in the gulf.

Making sure he wasn't being followed by either of the two crewmen or the American, the captain slipped into his cabin and turned on the small shortwave transceiver sitting on a table.

While it was warming up, he checked his wristwatch for the time. Perfect. Only a minute remained before he was due to send the message. He counted the seconds as the hand moved slowly around the face of the clock, then leaned forward and spoke into the small microphone.

The message would be received in Malivadi, on Mannar Island, from where it would be forwarded to Jaffna.

The captain turned off the set and leaned back in the chair, feeling relaxed and satisfied. He reached into his pocket and treated himself to a rare pleasure, one of the British cigarettes purchased in India.

As he inhaled the delicate perfume of the tobacco, he became too preoccupied with thoughts of how he would spend the money to hear the door behind open until it was too late.

Spinning in his chair, he saw the shadow of a man holding a silenced submachine gun. Before he could grab the fully loaded Tokarev pistol on the table near him, the shadowy figure squeezed the trigger and sprayed the captain with a continuous wave of lead until the walls of the small cabin were stained with blood and torn bits of tissue.

Carefully working his way past the widening pool of blood that covered the floor, the mustached mate held the subgun ready to fire as he leaned over and turned on the transmitter. He changed the setting on the dial, then squeezed the button on the microphone and gave his report in the soft accent of Indian Tamils. He listened for the brief acknowledgment, then turned to leave, knowing his message would be passed along until it reached the Tamil chieftain.

The sour-faced sailor didn't know why Thamby wanted the captain killed. He really didn't care. Rajiv Thamby was the leader and made the decisions. All he did was carry out the orders.

Now he had to take care of the American. The mate checked his weapon's magazine. It was almost empty. He dropped the clip to the floor of the cabin and snapped in a fresh one. Now he was ready to complete his assignment.

RAJIV THAMBY WAS expecting his two coleaders to arrive at his camp the following morning. The prospect infuriated him. He had done all the legwork, contacting suppliers, finding money to pay for the arms, and now Neelan and Konamalai wanted an equal share of the weapons and ammunition stored in the camp warehouse.

It had been a week of hell so far. The death of Madi Kirbal still angered him, and the cruelty that preceded his sister's suicide had opened scars of hate for the Sinhalese and their allies—such as the American diplomat locked in his cell, and the other American, the one who had come to rescue him.

They and others like them would do anything to appease the Sri Lankan government, even provide them with the tools to murder many more innocent Tamil men, women and children.

At least the mercenary sent by the Americans would soon be dead. His own man would make sure of that. And if the American government didn't ransom their representative with arms, he would be buried next to the other American.

He had made that point again when he had the negotiator dragged from his cell several hours earlier.

"Your time is running out," he had warned. "Our patience is coming to an end, American."

Filthy from the dirt that hung like a dark cloud in the cell, John Vu had no answer to give. All he wanted was a bath and sleep, neither of which he'd had since being taken prisoner.

"I wish the three of you would understand that I came here on my own to help you find peace," the exhausted man said quietly.

"The three of us?"

"I meant the other two men with whom you command the Tiger movement," Vu tried to explain.

"I run the LTTE," Thamby snapped.

Something in the American's attitude had angered the Tiger chieftain.

"The other two you refer to are not important. It takes a strong, dedicated leader to stand up to the world. Do you understand?"

Thamby waited for the American to reply. When he remained silent, the Tamil signaled for a guard to return the prisoner to his cell.

"If in twenty hours we receive no commitment from your government, you will die," he threatened.

The American government would give in to his demands. It was just a matter of letting them find some face-saving way to do it.

He had more pressing things on his mind, such as the cavalier attitude of the other two Tamil chieftains. The following day they would drive in with their men and expect Thamby to fill their trucks with the precious inventory in the warehouse.

Perhaps, he began to believe, it would be better for the Tiger cause if there were only one commander, instead of three.

SOMETHING WAS WRONG. Bolan could feel strong warning vibrations every time the mate passed him.

The captain had been missing for almost a half hour. In response to his question about where the skipper was, the mate had said the captain had suddenly become ill, and offered his assistance if Bolan had some need.

Even with the breeze masking noises, the soldier knew someone was creeping up behind him. Crew member or first mate, the Executioner got ready for him.

Easing the razor-sharp blade from its sheath, he wrapped his hand around the flat handle and let his arm hang by his side.

He could hear muffled breathing directly behind him, as if someone was unsuccessfully trying to hold his breath.

Whirling, he saw one of the crew raise a small ax. Bolan locked a foot behind the man's leg and pushed him backward. Suddenly off balance, the assailant fell to the deck, then struggled to his feet.

The Executioner rushed to him and slid the blade between two ribs before the man could push him away. Then he twisted the knife and pushed it up until he felt a momentary resistance. Pushing harder, he felt the resistance collapse.

Beneath him the crewman stiffened for a few seconds, then relaxed and stared past Bolan into space.

Looking up and past the body, the soldier saw the second member of the crew charging at him with a shouldered AK-47.

Throwing himself behind a bulkhead, Bolan retrieved the .44-caliber Desert Eagle from his belt, then moved out into the open and pumped two shots at the advancing attacker.

The rounds tore through space, then ground into the charger's midsection.

A stunned expression washed over the crewman's face as tissue and splintered bones gushed from his body in a sudden river of blood.

Two down. One to go.

The Executioner started the search for the rest of the crew.

The deck was empty, except for coils of rope and unswept garbage. He gripped the Desert Eagle and cautiously opened the door to the captain's cabin.

The floor was covered with blood, and lying on top of the drying pool was a body. The soldier kneeled

beside the body and turned it over. The expressionless
face of the captain stared up at him.

"Now it is your turn, American," a voice called
out.

Bolan turned his head and saw the first mate holding
a subgun.

"The gun. Drop it," the first mate ordered.

The big American obeyed and let the weapon fall
to the floor.

"Now out on the deck."

The soldier got to his feet and preceded the armed
sailor to the open deck.

"Who hired you?" Bolan asked.

"Not that it matters, but no one hired me. This was
the assignment my commander gave me."

There were few options available, the Executioner
decided, and only one that had even the remotest
chance of success.

Moving backward toward the rail, he waited for the
right moment, then threw himself over the side.

Surprised at the suicidal move, the Tiger hit man
rushed to the railing and leaned over.

Just below the railing, the Executioner was gripping
the anchor rope with one hand. Infuriated, the first
mate leaned out farther and pointed his subgun at the
American.

Summoning all his strength, Bolan pulled himself
up and grabbed the sailor by the throat. The man tried
to pull away, but the soldier kept increasing the pressure.

Dropping the gun into the water, the Tiger assassin
grabbed at Bolan's hand and tried to tear it away. The
Executioner continued to increase the pressure, forcing
a thumb against the carotid artery.

The American began to become a blur as the first mate found his hands less willing to fight back.

Suddenly his body gave up its efforts to fight. Falling to the deck, the first mate saw the huge foreigner follow him and wrap his arms around his head, then twist until the bones inside his neck exploded.

After that the first mate saw nothing.

23

Chandra Sirindikha refused to budge. For more than an hour she had argued with the ambassador about providing her with transportation. For an hour he kept refusing.

"I don't know who you think you are, Ms. Sirindikha, but we do not provide employees with government equipment just because they ask for it."

The young woman had anticipated the reaction. The message she had left for her superior in Washington, D.C., should have reached him by now.

The phone on the ambassador's desk rang, but he ignored it. "I believe Sri Lanka is your first assignment out of the United States. You have a lot to learn about how a State Department employee is expected to behave." The phone rang again. "We will continue this conversation after I take this call," the elegantly dressed man sitting behind the large desk said, signaling her to leave.

Frustrated, Sirindikha left the office and went back to her small cubicle in the communications section of the embassy. A few minutes later the ambassador, his face flushed with embarrassment, stood near her small desk.

"I didn't know," he began haltingly, trying to

frame an apology. "Would you come back to my office?"

The woman felt vindicated. Her superior had to have responded to her call.

BOLAN EASED the fishing boat against the wooden dock. Dropping his canvas bag on the warped planks, he opened it and found what he was seeking, then returned to the vessel.

The engine was still running. The soldier swung the boat around, pointing it toward the open water, then anchored the wheel with a rope.

The bodies were still where he had left them, but not for long, he reminded himself as he pressed a wedge of C-4 plastique to the main fuel tank. He then attached a detonator and timer, set to trigger the plastic explosive in a hour.

Bolan rammed the engine lever to its top speed, then raced to the bow and jumped onto the dock as the fishing boat began its last voyage.

Watching until the vessel vanished into the mist that hung over the Gulf of Mannar, the soldier turned away and lifted his canvas carryall.

There was a small, elderly Tamil waiting at the end of the dock. He looked different than the others Bolan had encountered. This man wore the black garb and collar of a Roman Catholic priest.

"Mr. Belasko?"

Bolan nodded. This had to be Sirindikha's contact.

"I am Father Tomas. I have a car parked nearby." Without waiting for acknowledgment, he turned and led Bolan down a narrow alley.

The parked car was ancient. It had once been a British-built Armstrong, a pre-World War II relic of a time when England had a thriving automotive industry. Sixty years later a great number of mechanics had been inventive in their efforts to keep the vehicle functional with body parts scrounged from auto wreckers. It looked more like a cartoon caricature of a car than an actual automobile, and Bolan wondered if it really ran.

The priest saw the soldier's skeptical stare.

"Yes, it does run," Father Tomas said, smiling. "Sometimes I think it is a miracle that it does. But miracles do happen."

Dropping his bag on the back seat, Bolan got in on the passenger side and waited for the priest to start the engine.

A small series of muffled explosions rumbled from beneath the hood as the small man pumped the gas. Finally the engine surrendered and kicked over.

"Where is the woman who contacted me? I thought she was coming with you."

"It would take too long to explain," Bolan replied.

"We can talk when we get to my humble home," the priest said, then added, "The woman asked if I could find you transportation." He shrugged. "Unfortunately we no longer have car-hire agencies in Jaffna. But you are more than welcome to use my humble vehicle."

"Thanks."

He had driven worse. Not much worse, but worse.

THIS HAD BEEN Sirindikha's first field assignment. It was different than when she'd been in training. Shooting guns at fixed targets wasn't the same as firing at people who were shooting back. Until she arrived in Sri Lanka, she associated death with old age, illness and accidents. Since Belasko arrived, she had met death in a dozen or more forms.

Still, there was something about the man that was both appealing and frightening at the same time. She felt compelled to help him, even though he'd ordered her to stay in Colombo.

A question from the ambassador brought her back to the present. "What is it you need?" he asked.

"I'm not sure whether a powerboat or a helicopter would be more useful," she replied, thinking aloud. "Or perhaps both."

"To do what?"

"To rescue Bel—" She caught herself. The big American might need help, but she didn't think he needed to be rescued. She substituted another name. "To rescue Mr. Vu."

The ambassador looked surprised. "You know where he is being held?"

Nodding, she answered, "Yes, I think so."

"Shouldn't we wait for Washington to tell us what to do?"

"Not if you want to see Mr. Vu alive."

Disturbed that he was being asked to actively participate in a nondiplomatic action, the ambassador reluctantly made a decision.

"Decide what you need. I'll find a way to make it available."

THE TWO TAMIL LEADERS met at Neelan's base, just outside of Pooneryn, thirty miles south of Thamby's camp. A half-dozen large trucks, filled with Tiger guerrillas, waited while Neelan and Konamalai had a private conversation.

"Our brother has strange ideas about the revolution," Neelan commented.

"He's been fighting too long. I am not certain that he really wants to see an agreement to create a separate, autonomous Tamil region," Konamalai agreed.

"This latest reluctance to share the arms in his warehouse speaks ill for the future of the Tigers."

The eagle-beaked Tamil nodded. "We shall see how cooperative he is when we arrive at his camp."

Words poured from the Tamil with the large facial birthmark. "My men are well-armed. Just in case…"

"Wise. So are mine," the other leader replied, then looked at his wristwatch. It was time to leave for Kaitadi.

THE TAMIL PRIEST had cleared the dining table after sharing a meal with Bolan and spread open a map. Pointing to a spot twenty miles northeast of the city, he commented, "This is one of Thamby's camps. Kaitadi. It's where he stores his arms and supplies. It was once a village of farmers. Now it contains at least thirty men trained to kill."

"Where is Thamby's hut? Where does he keep his prisoners?"

Father Tomas searched through a drawer in a small chest and found a faded photograph, which he placed on top of the map.

The priest was standing next to a tall, hard-faced man. Behind them was a large structure. He pointed to the building behind him. "This is the camp warehouse. Next to it is where Thamby lives and works."

"And the prisoners' quarters?"

"Mostly they are chained to metal poles in the

warehouse. There is no need for cells, since none of them live very long.''

Bolan understood. It was cheaper to kill a prisoner than to feed and clothe him.

''What about the American you reported they had captured?''

''For some reason they have let him live. He is being kept in a small room with barred windows next door to Rajiv Thamby's quarters. But,'' he warned, ''guards watch him twenty-four hours a day.''

Bolan had one more question he needed answered. ''Why are you turning against your own people?''

''In the photograph I showed you, I stood close to Thamby. We were even closer in real life. He and his partners were idealists. So was I.

''When the STF or the police came looking for him, he and the others would run to this rectory to hide.''

The priest led the way to the closet, then opened the door. Pulling out Bolan's bag, he kneeled and pulled up a false floor panel. ''They would hide in the small room beneath the rectory until the authorities finally left in frustration. We had a common goal. The Tamil people would become independent and whole again.''

Father Tomas's shoulders slumped. Once again he became the disillusioned Roman Catholic priest.

''Everything has changed. Perhaps not Konamalai, but the other two have. All they seek now is personal power. Someplace along the journey, the Tamil people were forgotten.''

''You could be killed for your views,'' Bolan warned.

''Too many have already been killed without a good

reason. At least if I go, it will be for something in which I believe.''

A knock at the front door of the small house stopped the conversation. Bolan took the Beretta from under his jacket and signaled for the priest to open the door.

24

Chandra Sirindikha, dressed in jeans and a light blue work shirt, stood on the doorstep.

"Can I come in?" she asked.

Bolan eased his hand from the butt of the Beretta. "What are you doing here?"

"I thought you might like some company," the woman replied, trying to sound casual.

The soldier was about to reply when he realized that something bothered him about the woman's sudden appearance.

"How did you get here?"

"The ambassador was kind enough to give me a lift here in one of the embassy helicopters."

Bolan's respect for the Fresno-born woman grew. As difficult as she seemed, she was also resourceful.

He introduced her to the priest.

Father Tomas recognized her voice. "Ah, the woman I spoke to on the telephone. The woman who does research for the American government."

"Actually that's not my real job," Sirindikha said apologetically.

"CIA?" Bolan asked.

"Not quite. State Department Intelligence and Research Service." Then she added, "After all, Mr. Vu was a senior diplomat before he resigned. We like to take care of our own. And since you don't speak either Sinhalese or Tamil, Mr. Belasko, and I do, I felt I might be useful.''

"I may be paranoid, but I think the risk is too great for you to get involved," Bolan warned.

"Even paranoids have enemies, and need all the help they can get," Father Tomas commented.

"It will be dark in a few hours," the priest warned. "I will guide you until you are on the correct road leading out of the city."

Sirindikha was curious. "How will you get back?"

"We still have buses, and I might even run into a parishioner returning from a drive in the country."

BOLAN DROVE the borrowed Armstrong while his companion reloaded her H&K P-5.

"Be sure to fill several magazines just in case you need them," he told her.

The young woman nodded her agreement as she concentrated on pushing rounds into the metal magazine. The ancient vehicle kept bouncing on the potholed street.

"Could you keep this pile of junk level? I feel like I'm dancing the rumba sitting down."

"Tell it to the gravel road," Bolan replied.

Father Tomas, sitting in the back, offered an apology. "Once Jaffna had excellent roads and streets filled with tourists."

"This old tub has seen better days," the young woman commented.

"I agree," the priest replied. "But this old girl can still get me to where I need to go."

Sirindikha looked embarrassed. "This is your car?"

"Yes," Father Tomas said. "But don't feel bad. I

trust her more than I would trust one of the new, un-feeling cars from Japan or the United States.''

Minutes later the priest tapped Bolan on the shoulder. "I'll get out here. If you follow this road, it will lead you out of the city. Stay on it for twenty miles and, just before you reach Kaitadi, you'll see a narrow dirt road on your right. Take that road and you'll reach the Tigers' camp.''

Bolan pulled over to the curb and watched as the fragile priest got out and started walking back in the direction of his church.

"WHAT KIND of problems do you think we're walking into?" Sirindikha asked.

"We'll find out soon enough," the Executioner predicted, then tried to dodge the potholes on the two-lane highway.

Except for an occasional animal that risked its well-being to cross in front of him, he had seen no signs of life. If it hadn't been for the frightened creatures, he would have sworn no living thing existed here.

Bolan slowed the vehicle as he saw the dirt road marked on his map. "Here we go," he announced.

"I'm ready," Sirindikha announced.

He turned the car into the narrow dirt road. The vehicle rolled and buckled as it bounced on the loose dirt. The bushes that lined both sides of the unpaved path scraped against the fenders.

Bolan glanced around. The fields looked to be starving for water. The thick dark clouds above, heavy with moisture, seemed like the answer to the local farmers' prayer.

What bothered the warrior was the lack of life in

and around Jaffna. Back in the rectory, the priest had explained that this was *poya*, a full-moon day.

"All Sri Lankan celebrate full-moon days. Especially when they fall on a Monday or Friday," Father Tomas had said. "We take our holidays very seriously. Between the religions there are nearly thirty holidays celebrated as official events. A full five-day work week is a comparative rarity."

But from his experience, Bolan knew that farmers rarely wandered very far from their fields. He wondered where they had gone.

The hazy outlines of small, one-story houses were ahead. Bolan knew this was the destination. In this village he was certain he would find John Vu. If death hadn't already claimed him.

Suddenly Bolan eased off on the gas pedal.

His companion looked at him. "Something wrong?"

"There's something up ahead," he announced. "We'll stop here and check it out."

Pulling the ancient car off the road, he picked up his Zeiss binoculars and studied the area in front of them. A large number of fatigue-clad men were gathered in the open area across from the warehouse. From what he could determine, the men were on a break, arm wrestling and gambling with dice.

The soldier decided he needed to get closer. Checking to make sure the Beretta and Desert Eagle had full magazines, he grabbed the Uzi SMG and a handful of clips.

"Wait here," he told the woman. "I'm going to check out the area."

Without waiting for her agreement, Bolan moved toward the thick foliage.

"How long do I wait for you to come back?"

"No more than an hour," the big American replied. "If I'm not back by then, or you hear shots, get the hell out of here."

The Executioner decided to scout the village before taking action. Father Tomas had said John Vu was being held in a small hut next to the one the Tamil leader occupied.

The problem was that Bolan didn't know which of the several dozen buildings was Vu's prison.

A moment later it didn't matter to him—he felt the butt end of a rifle smash down on the back of his skull, and then there was only darkness.

25

Inside the warehouse Bolan struggled to force his eyes open. The throbbing in his head racked him with pain. Everything seemed blurry.

As the fog lifted from his eyes, the soldier remembered that he had been struck from behind. He could feel the thick blood oozing from an open scalp wound.

He tried to move, then looked down and saw the handcuffs that fastened him to a heavy vertical support pipe. There was no way he could open them without the key.

Bolan looked around the large open space. Dozens of opened wooden crates were stacked everywhere, and he could smell the aroma of the oil-saturated packing material that lined the weapons boxes.

He wondered if the standpipe could be sawed through with the edge of the handcuffs. He began to rub his manacled wrists up and down the metal pipe, tearing into the skin around his wrists each time he moved. His efforts might prove useless, but he had to try. The alternative was death at the hands of the Tamil terrorists.

THAMBY EXPLODED in anger when his aide, Lalith, told him that the guards captured a stranger and handcuffed him to a vertical pipe inside the warehouse.

"Why didn't they just kill him?"

"I was going to tell them to do exactly that. But you know how you get if we do something without your knowing," the man replied nervously.

The Tiger commander was about to issue an order when the sound of vehicles interrupted him. He looked up and saw a pair of Land Rovers leading large trucks into the village. The convoy pulled up to the building and stopped.

Thamby turned to Lalith. "We will get rid of him as soon as they leave," he muttered, then walked over to greet the arrivals.

Forcing himself to be pleasant, the Tamil chieftain embraced each of the other two leaders.

"Let's have a look at the cache of arms we'll be sharing," he announced in a jovial-sounding tone.

Thamby was about to lead the other two into the warehouse when Lalith leaned over and whispered in his ear. "Don't forget we got that stranger inside."

The Tiger commander had forgotten. Quickly he made a decision.

"You and some of the other men haul out a case of guns and a case of ammunition," he instructed his aide.

Looking at Neelan and Konamalai, he added, "You can inspect them outside just as easily as in that hot, stuffy building. And I know you'll want to test them, too, so we might as well do it all out here."

Neelan looked around the area. "And nobody will hear the shots?"

"No," Thamby replied. "There's nobody around for miles."

One of the guards drove a yellow forklift out of the warehouse. He had already opened the two cases perched on the front end. Thamby reached into the top case, pulled out an M-16 A-2 and handed it to Konamalai.

He wondered if either of the two Tamil leaders remembered his conversation about the former KMS trainer and the cargo of arms he was offering for sale.

"Finest weapon the U.S. Army's ever produced. Relatively light, accurate and it can empty a 30-round clip in seconds. Not only that, it doesn't jam like the Chinese weapons. And it cost the LTTE nothing."

"Nothing?"

One of his men had found Atwater's body when he came to deliver the advance payments. Leaving as quickly as he had arrived, the messenger returned the money to Thamby.

The Tigers had accepted the cargo delivered to the Jaffna docks, then killed all the members of the crew before loading the arms onto waiting trucks for transport to the warehouse.

The newspapers had credited the incident to some battle for control of the Jaffna waterfront by different gangs.

The tall, thin Tamil studied the assault rifle, then handed it to the third leader of the Tiger command. Neelan balanced the weapon in his right hand, then looked at Thamby. "You say it is accurate?"

"One of the most accurate at fifty yards." He pointed to a teak tree. "That tree is just about fifty yards away. Try it yourself."

He reached into the case of ammunition and grabbed a handful of rounds. "We have clips for them inside, but you can single load them for testing."

The Tamil area leader gestured for one of his men to join him. He handed the assault rifle to the slender, grim-looking man and pointed to the tree. The gunman took the rounds from Thamby and shoved one into the firing chamber. Aiming carefully, he squeezed the trigger. The bullet chopped away a large wedge of wood from the trunk of the tree.

The Tiger commander told one of his men to get a handful of clips and fill them.

He turned to the two visitors. "Why don't you have all of your men try them? I think they will prefer them to the AK-47s."

Neelan glanced at the other visitor. "Why not?"

Thamby's aide pulled him aside. "I thought you were opposed to sharing our warehouse with the others?"

The Tamil commander smiled. "Soldiers are loyal to those who provide them with the best weapons. If this has to become a confrontation, I want all of the Tigers siding with me," he replied in a quiet voice.

Two of the guerrillas were busy filling two dozen clips with ammunition.

With a nod of approval from the two visitors, their men each grabbed a rifle and loaded it. At first they were satisfied to shoot at the tree, then one of Konamalai's men challenged one of Neelan's to a contest.

Neelan walked over to Thamby. "Do you have any paper targets?"

Thamby shook his head. One of his men leaned over and whispered, "How about that prisoner inside?"

The Tiger chieftain's eyes lit up for a moment as he considered the idea, then reconsidered. He wasn't sure how the visitors would feel about using a human target.

"We'll take care of him later. Go inside and bring

out some crate covers, and find something to paint circles on them.''

The testing of the M-16s had turned into a shooting party. Konamalai's men kept throwing money onto a pile as they bet Neelan's troops they could outshoot them.

In a mixture of English and Sinhalese, the rebels tried to outbrag each other. First, two of Konamalai's fighters stood behind the line drawn in the dirt and fired three rounds at a painted crate cover.

Lalith had agreed to act as both range officer and judge. ''Two hits on the edge of the outer circle,'' he yelled.

The Tamil who had just fired the weapon gave the rest of his men a thumbs-up gesture as he stepped away from the firing line.

Two of Neelan's rebels were next. Standing a few feet apart, they aimed the assault rifles and fired a pair of shots, then stepped back. The aide walked over and examined the wooden target.

''One inside the outer ring. The other's a bull's-eye,'' he shouted.

The two shooters slapped palms and walked away.

Until then, Neelan and Konamalai had kept in the background, content to watch their men testing the new weapons. As the competition between the two groups grew more hostile, they began to edge closer to the firing line.

Before long, the two leaders were egging their men on to achieve greater accuracy.

''A bonus of a hundred rupees for every bull's-eye you get,'' Neelan announced to his troops.

Konamalai stared at him, then turned to his men and

offered double that each time the center of the target was hit.

Neelan smiled at him. In a sarcastic tone of voice, he asked, "You don't really believe your men could beat in a shooting contest one of the men I have trained?"

"These are men I have personally picked. They would die for me. Your men are trained like the cobra that kills for the pleasure of killing. Loyalty will always win in the end."

"Willing to put your money where your mouth is?"

"As much as you care to lose."

"Let's make it a friendly bet," Neelan said, sounding confident. "You name the amount."

"Five thousand rupees, if you're not afraid to lose that much," the other Tamil chief growled.

"It is a wager."

Watching them, Thamby turned to his aide. "Sooner or later their men are going to become tired of being used as pawns in a personal feud. Then I will step in." He looked around. "Right now we need some more magazines."

Lalith turned to the guard, took his ring of keys and walked into the warehouse.

BOLAN HAD PAUSED in his efforts, listening to the gunshots from outside the warehouse. He looked at his wrists. They had become swollen from the constant rubbing against the cuffs, and the dried blood that filled his open wounds felt like sandpaper every time he moved his hands.

He could hear the footsteps of someone approaching him and slid to the ground. If the Tamil came close enough, perhaps he could trip him, then take him out of action.

Breathing deeply, Bolan closed his eyes and let his body relax. Then he opened his eyes and glanced at the man walking in his direction. Closing his eyes again, Bolan pretended to be asleep.

Lalith glanced at the chained figure slumped on the floor. The cases he was looking for were stacked just behind the sleeping man. The aide started to step over the figure when he felt himself losing balance.

Bolan had locked his legs around the right knee of the terrorist and twisted quickly. As the aide tried to struggle to his feet, the soldier rammed the tip of his left foot into the man's crotch.

Grunting with pain, the Tamil reached for his injured genitals. The big American knew the man would start to shout for help, so he had to quickly silence him. He locked his feet around his adversary's neck and began to squeeze.

He lifted his head and watched his enemy's face flush as Bolan's feet crushed his windpipe. The rebel tried to tear Bolan's viselike feet from his throat, fighting for survival.

The soldier's feet were like clamps. Nothing could force them to release their hold. Bolan saw the man's face darken into a thin purple color, and the Tamil suddenly gave up the struggle. His head lolled to one side.

Exhausted, Bolan let himself fall backward and rested for a moment.

Thamby shouted into the warehouse, "We need those magazines out here."

Using his feet to pull the body of the dead man closer, the soldier twisted his own body so he could use his manacled hands to search through the Tamil's clothes.

He found a key chain in one of the rear pockets of his pants. Bolan picked it up and searched through the various keys until he found the one he knew would open his handcuffs.

Twisting his arms, he carefully inserted the key into the handcuff opening and tried to push it in.

The set of keys fell to the ground. Frustrated, he tried again, this time twisting his hands to make it easier to reach the handcuffs' keyhole. He forced himself to ignore the excruciating pain of the raw wounds around his wrists as he again inserted the key.

Turning it carefully, he felt the subtle click that meant he was free. Quickly Bolan opened the other cuff and stood. He searched the immediate area for a weapon. He needed something powerful. He looked into an open crate and grabbed one of the M-16 A-2s. A full case of M-203 grenade launchers had been opened.

Bolan fit one of them under the assault rifle and picked up a half-dozen 40 mm frag grenades. Loading one into the M-203, the Executioner shoved the rest into the baggy pockets of his battle fatigue uniform. Continuing his search, he found four empty clips and a case of metal-jacketed 5.56 mm ammunition.

The soldier knew that somebody would be coming to look for the missing terrorist, but he knew he had to take the time to fill the clips if he wanted to survive. One by one he pushed the rounds down on the spring inside each clip until all four were fully loaded. Grabbing a handful of ammunition, he pushed one into the firing chamber and shoved the rest into one of his pockets, then clicked a magazine into the assault rifle and moved to the front door.

Now he was ready. He wasn't sure how many men there were outside, or how well they could fight.

But he was determined that John Vu would be rescued.

26

The sound of rifle fire frustrated the State Department Intelligence agent. She wasn't sure who was doing the shooting, the American or the Tigers.

Sirindikha checked the magazine in the P-5, which was full, and decided Belasko needed help.

Then she looked at the autoloader in her hands. It didn't seem as if it was enough firepower to help the man fight off a couple dozen or more guerrillas.

What else did she have?

She saw the canvas bag Belasko had brought with him. Perhaps there were things inside she could use.

Digging through the bag, she found several grenades clustered in one of the corners. She grabbed three and shoved them into her pockets.

The M-16 assault rifle caught her eye. At a little over three feet in length, the powerful gun looked intimidating. But when she lifted it, the weapon felt lighter than she'd expected.

Raising it to her shoulder, she found she could lean her cheek against the stock and aim with the aid of the simple sights. It wasn't her first choice. She would have preferred to carry the stubby Uzi Belasko had carried. But the M-16 was the most powerful weapon she could find.

Grabbing some clips, she snapped a 30-round magazine into the M-16 and shoved the remaining three into her work-shirt pockets, then set off on foot to join the battle.

As HE WATCHED the shooting match from the cover of the shaded entrance to the warehouse, Bolan knew he was no match for thirty trained and armed guerrillas. He needed a distraction, something that would send the terrorists running in panic.

He looked down at the combo weapon in his hand, then aimed the launcher at where a dozen of the men were involved in a shooting competition and squeezed the trigger.

The soldier watched as the grenade twisted a path toward the cluster of armed men. It landed just in front of them, scattering bits of fury-driven metal in every direction.

Two men fell to the ground as slivers of metal sliced through their skulls and into their brains. Three more terrorists screamed with pain as shards of metal tore into their stomachs and chests. Clutching their wounds, they fell to the ground.

Panic took over the competing riflemen. The seven who hadn't been killed or seriously wounded kept turning to see where the grenade had come from. They didn't have to wait long. Bolan released another missile, aiming this time at where the vehicles were parked.

Flames burst from ruptured gas tanks. The only escape for the gunmen would be on foot.

Some of the Tigers had already begun to edge toward the far end of the camp.

The soldier worked his way around the warehouse

until he was fifty yards away, then reloaded the launcher.

He released the bomb, aiming for the wide-open doors of the warehouse, and covered his head as the muffled rumblings became a massive explosion that threw chunks of the roof and metal siding thirty feet up into the sky.

Explosion followed explosion as detonated ammunition and grenades ignited more ammunition and grenades. The ground rocked as flames and explosions consumed what was left of the storage building.

For fifteen of the terrorists, the disintegration of the warehouse was the final push. Taking off on foot, they began to race in a panic down the dirt street, in the direction of the farmland north of the Tiger base.

Bolan moved into the open, spraying 3-round bursts at the men in front of him. Two soldiers fell before they could turn their weapons on him.

The eagle-beaked Tamil whom Bolan recognized as one of the Tiger leaders rallied three of his men to charge the Executioner. They fired wildly, their shots tearing into huts and burning vehicles.

Bolan had twisted out of the path of the bullets. One of them barely missed the fleshy part of his upper arm as he snapped off a pair of rounds at the Tamil leader.

Two of the bullets shattered the other man's shoulder and shoved the guerrilla leader back into a pile of metal fragments from the decimated warehouse.

Staggered from the wound, Konamalai turned and ran behind a wall of terrorists, all trying to target the attacker with slugs from their assault rifles.

Bolan dived to the ground and kept his head down as lead tore through the air inches above him.

Resting the M-16 on the ground, the Executioner

waited until the five gunners who rushed him got closer, then hosed them with a continuous stream of lead.

Two rounds stole the life of their leader, Neelan. With a look of surprise permanently imprinted on his face, the Tamil sank to his knees, then fell on his face.

The five terrorists stopped in their tracks and made the fatal error of looking back as their leader fell to the ground. The Executioner took them out of play with one sweeping burst.

Bolan pulled himself to his feet, then saw Thamby standing in front of him, his face twisted by anger, his hands locked around a 9 mm Skorpion subgun.

There was no time to wonder where the Tiger chieftain had been hiding during the battle, and barely enough time to try to fight back.

"You will die, American, and the man you came to save will die after you do."

The Tamil leader glanced at the still forms of the two men who had been his partners. "I was planning to kill them anyway, so you did me a favor. There never was room for more than one leader in the movement."

Bolan knew there was nothing he could say—or wanted to say—to stop the Tamil from trying to empty his weapon into him.

"Sooner or later," the Executioner said coldly, "someone will come along and take you down."

There was movement behind Thamby. Bolan had tried to keep Thamby distracted. Now the soldier looked beyond the Tamil chieftain.

"An old trick," the terrorist leader commented cynically. "There is no one behind me."

"Yes, there is," a voice replied from a distance.

Chandra Sirindikha squeezed the trigger of the M-16 A-2 and kept firing until the recoil pushed her backward to the ground.

The Tamil terrorist half turned to stare at his killer, and raised his subgun to fire back.

Despite the large piece of flesh missing from his right side, chewed away by 5.56 mm rounds, Thamby began to fire the Skorpion at the fallen woman.

The pain he felt made his aim less accurate. Lead tore into the dirt until finally two rounds carved their way into the female fighter's midsection.

Bolan raised the rifle in his hand and squeezed off a round. The hollow clicking of metal on metal was ominous.

Fear replaced the expression of anger on Thamby's face. Despite the blood running from his side, he was able to turn and run.

Bolan took off after him, searching his pockets for a replacement magazine as he did. Finally the soldier had to stop to eject the empty clip and replace it.

The sound of an engine starting up disturbed the quiet. The Tamil was behind the wheel of a Land Rover, focusing his attention on escape. Bolan tried to use his body to stop him, but Thamby twisted the wheel in panic and raced around him and down the street in the direction of Jaffna.

The Executioner turned to check on the young woman when he heard someone call from inside the cell.

The accent was American.

Bolan shattered the lock of the door with a round from his M-16, then kicked the heavy wooden barrier open.

The man who emerged looked exhausted and frightened. Even though the man had a three-day growth of beard, Bolan recognized John Vu.

At least one part of the mission was over. There still was one thing he had to do.

Bolan examined the diplomat with his eyes. "You okay?"

"Yes." Vu smiled and commented in a soft drawl, "I'd recognize that accent anywhere. New England?"

"Used to be," the soldier answered. "Want to stop to shave and change clothes before we head home?"

"Do you think we've got time?"

"We've got time. After we drop someone at the nearest hospital."

27

Bolan and the rescued American diplomat supported the young woman between them. Squeezed in the front seat of the priest's Armstrong, she let her head slump on the Executioner's shoulder. He kept assuring her they'd be at the hospital soon, but she didn't respond.

He repeated the promise.

Finally the woman opened her eyes. "Okay, okay. I heard you the first time."

"How do you feel, young lady?" Vu asked.

She tried to smile at him, but felt too weak to move her lips. Slowly turning to Bolan, she shook her head. "I don't think I like this part of the job," she said before fainting.

STOPPING LONG ENOUGH to have his wrists bandaged and his scalp wound cleaned up, the Executioner left Sirindikha and Vu in the care of the doctors at Jaffna General Hospital.

He had to look for someone, and he had an idea where he might find him.

After parking the ancient car at the curb outside Father Tomas's church, Bolan grabbed his retrieved Uzi submachine gun and checked the front door of the rectory.

As he suspected, it was locked. The old priest wouldn't have had time to return yet.

Walking around to the rear, he found a small window and forced it open with the edge of his combat knife.

He eased his way inside and found himself in a tiny bedroom. Except for the crucifix on the wall above the narrow bed, the room was bare.

The door to the living room was ajar. The strong scent of curry spices filled his nostrils, reminding him of the potent meal the priest had served him.

A tall man sat at the tiny dining table, his back to Bolan. Dishes of curry and bowls of rice sat in front of him.

The soldier was tempted to end it now, but a personal moral code stopped him from shooting a man in the back.

"Thamby," he called out.

The figure continued to eat.

"It's all over," he shouted.

The man seemed frozen. Bolan moved closer.

Suddenly Thamby turned and snapped off a pair of rounds from the pistol he gripped in his right hand.

One of the slugs whispered across the soldier's left cheekbone, startling him for a moment.

The Executioner regained his balance and spewed a wave of bullets at where the Tamil had been sitting.

Thamby had thrown himself to one side, and the slugs tore into the far wall behind the dining table.

Bolan charged at the terrorist, spraying the area in front of him with a sustained burst of death.

Two slugs chewed into Thamby's shoulder and knocked the autoloader from his grasp. The Tamil grabbed a long knife from the dining table and threw himself at his enemy. Arms locked in midair, the two men struggled for the upper hand.

The Executioner tried to raise the Uzi, but Thamby's powerful grip forced the weapon down to Bolan's side.

The Tamil lifted the knife high in the air as if he were offering some hellish demon of his own devising a human sacrifice.

Forcing up the Uzi inch by inch, the Executioner felt its muzzle snag on the belt around Thamby's pants, the ensuing loud explosion temporarily deafening him. He felt himself being shoved backward by the recoil of the gun.

For a moment Bolan thought that somehow he had missed him. Then he saw the cavity in the Tamil's midsection. Blood and bits of tissue began to ooze from the giant wound.

Thamby's hand was still curled around the long knife, and, despite the agony reflected in his expression, the Tiger terrorist raised the blade.

Bolan did the only thing he could. He fired at point-blank range, nearly cutting his enemy in two. Thamby fell to the wooden floor, his lifeblood staining the planks dark red.

Outside, the rains had finally come, a gentle stream of water washing the streets of Jaffna. Soon, Bolan knew, the stream would turn to a torrent.

Opening the door, the Executioner left the small house and walked into fresh air and life.

EPILOGUE

Mack Bolan sat in the metal chair next to the hospital bed and looked at the young woman who huddled under the covers. The doctors had removed the life-support equipment and replaced it with an IV antibiotic drip.

He waited until she opened her eyes.

When she did, she smiled. "I don't like this part of the job, either," she said in a whisper.

"You could go back to being a communications clerk," he suggested.

She opened her eyes wide and in a mock tone of horror, replied, "And miss all the fun? Never."

Outside, the monsoon season had finally arrived. Sheets of rain tumbled from the dark, cloudy sky.

Sirindikha listened to the storm for a moment, then turned and looked at Bolan. "Where do you go now?"

"Home with John Vu," he replied.

The soft but determined voice behind them added his own comment.

"John Vu isn't going home. Not yet."

The soldier turned and glanced at the diplomat, who had quietly entered the hospital room.

"Any reason?"

"That Konamalai chap. According to the doctor who checked him out, he's got some holes in him, but nothing that won't heal. I've been talking to him."

He shook his head. "He isn't a bad fellow to do business with. My guess is that he'd like to find an answer that would stop the killings and give the Tamils a place of their own. Now that he's kind of in charge of these Tigers, we agreed that when he's up and around, we'd get together and do some more talking."

Bolan felt it necessary to remind Vu that the Tigers weren't the only ones in the war. "Will the Sri Lankan government accept a settlement?"

"Nice thing about us is that we take care of our friends. I think the government will get the message."

"Then what?"

"Then I go home and start to enjoy my retirement."

Bolan nodded as a hint of a smile played on his lips.

Vu looked at the Executioner. "What about you?"

"My mission is accomplished."

"Will I ever see you again?"

"You never know," he replied.